Slowly, slowly I move, until my hand is outstretched towards her. She leans forward, sniffs my fingers. Her muzzle is soft, her whiskers tickle, her breath is quick and warm. She licks my hand; I am singing inside, for joy. Then she turns aside, sniffs the grass about my fishing place, and gulps down the salmon that is Morag's. She examines the line and hook, then moves to go.

I stand up, longing for her to stay. "You were mother and father to me," I say.

The she-wolf turns again, her head dark now in the twilight. Her breath steams in the cool air, and tiny insects dance above her. She smells of earth and summer wind.

Sherryl Jordan has written a number of award-winning novels for young adults. She lives with her husband in Tauranga, New Zealand.

Wolf-Woman

Sherryl Jordan

Wolf-Woman

Sherryl Jordan

Published by
Bantam Doubleday Dell Books for Young Readers
a division of
Bantam Doubleday Dell Publishing Group, Inc.
1540 Broadway
New York, New York 10036

ISBN: 0-440-21969-8

RL: 6.2

Reprinted by arrangement with Houghton
Mifflin Company

Printed in the United States of America

July 1996

10 9 8 7 6 5 4 3 2 1

OPM

For Lee and Kym
with love

*

and in memory
of Kama,
who taught me that
animals have souls

1

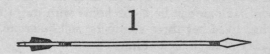

We chose each other, the wolves and I, though our first meeting is so far back in my life that it is lost in the shades of memory, and I have only the story the chieftain told, who took me from the wolves and let me live for a time with his people. I treasured his words about my strange beginnings, for wolves have walked through all my dreams, and always their moon-drowned howls have haunted me.

Ahearn is our chieftain's name. I call him my chieftain too, though he and all his clan have hair as gold as harvest-wheat, while I alone have hair of black. I come from a race that is enemy to his, and it is only by Ahearn's word that I am permitted to live with his clan. Even his word is tested at times, and my life hangs in a fearful balance between his people's suspicion and his care for me.

.I cannot say he loves me, for he loves no one but his first wife, Nolwynn. He had a daughter once, whom he adored. But his daughter drowned in a river during a storm, and his wife hurt her back when she swam against the raging torrents to try to save her child. Since that time Nolwynn has lain in her bed, unable to move her legs. The wife of any other man would have been put to death as a kindness, and to spare the clan useless work. But Ahearn forbade her death, and looked after her himself, and mourned for his daughter.

Then late one day he came home with me, a child who had lived but three summers, and he swore that the gods had given me to him.

I remember well the story he told, for he told it many times. I remember a night in my second winter in his house. It was a special night for story-telling, for we had, as honoured guest, the bard whose name is Camelin. He sometimes came to visit us, on his journeys through our lands. Camelin tells stories and sings songs at all the villages. He is a respected poet and entertainer, and the bringer of news from far places.

On that wintry night of his visit, all the men and women of the clan were gathered on the earthen floor about Ahearn's fire, laughing and drinking. I remember the stifling heat, and the rich smell of roasted pork, and the odour of leather boots and fur. The men wore brightly coloured tunics, and their flaxen hair was long and shining on their dark fur cloaks. The scabbards of their swords and their jewelled brooches and buckles glinted in the firelight.

I was standing on a stool by the window-hole, listening to the wolves howling in the snow. One of the women became angry with me, because she had told me to do something and I did not hear. She pulled me off the stool, and said I was a useless slave with no right to share the chieftain's house. I cried, because I was old enough then to understand.

Ahearn reproached her, saying I was not a slave, and gave me to Nolwynn to be soothed. When he went back to the fire Camelin asked him how a dark-haired child came to be living in his house.

"It is a story of loss and pain," said Ahearn, "but I will tell it."

The clan fell silent when Ahearn began; and I still can feel the warmth of Nolwynn's furs, and the comfort of her hand resting on my hair.

"My heart was sore, in those days," said Ahearn. "I thought that I had angered the gods by loving my daughter more than I loved them; and I believed they had taken her from me, in punishment. And so I resented the gods, wanted to shake my fist at them. In my rage I took my warriors into battle again and again, defying the gods to strike me down, to end my sorrow and my despair. But always we won, and I was never hurt. And before that last battle, that last of the bitter winter time, I swore that if I was victorious I would make my peace with the gods and with myself, and grieve no more.

"Again the fight was ours. A quick victory it was, for the enemy men were just back from a hunt, and the youths were cleaning the skin of a bear they had killed. The women were roasting the bear's meat, and the children were playing. They were dark-heads and spoke strange words such as madmen speak, and they were weak and undeserving of their land. We fell upon them like thunder, and slew them mightily.

"And on the way back we saw wolves on our forest path, and we lifted our bows and would have shot them for sport, for the blood lust was in us still; but we saw that with them was a human child. A girl-child. Her arm was about a she-wolf's neck, and she was calm and young, with a fearless look and eyes sea-green like my daughter's eyes. Like an omen she was, a sign from the gods that they still favoured me.

"I told my men to kill the wolves, but to save her. The wolves were fierce in their defence of her, and would have torn us into pieces had we not been armed. When they all were dead we took the child from among them and brought her to our place. And she is become Tanith, adopted daughter to Nolwynn. When she is grown she will look after her new mother, and be a comfort to her. And Tanith is no slave, but a child of the wolves, and a member of my house."

There was a long silence when Ahearn finished his story. I remember watching the embers in the fire, and recalling, for a brief and joyful moment, the blazing of wolves' eyes in a dark den.

Then the bard left his place by Ahearn and came and sat by me. He took my hand in both of his, and I noticed how smooth his palms were, for he never worked in a field or held a weapon.

"I have a story for you, Tanith of the wolves," he said. His voice was deep and hushed, as if he told the tale for me alone, though all the clan was listening.

"It is a story of your dark-haired race. A story of their shamans, who are noble and wise. I know it is true, for I have talked with a dark-haired seer, at her fireside. She told me there are shamans who leave chosen babies outside the dens of wolves, so the children grow up understanding the ways and language of animals. The babes are left for only a few days, then gathered back to their clan. They grow up to become shamans themselves, far-sighted, and in harmony with the earth. It may be, Tanith, that you were one of those favoured ones."

"Not too favoured," said an elderly woman, "since her clan forgot to gather her back."

They all laughed, except Nolwynn and the bard.

"There are many reasons why the clan may have been prevented," Camelin said. "They might have been killed by sickness, or by warriors. Maybe the wolves moved to another territory, and took the child with them. But no matter how Tanith came to be with them, this we know: that the wolves looked after her well, and guarded and protected her."

"Until they met Ahearn's sword," said someone else.

There was laughter again, and the men began talking about dark-heads and the cunning of evil beasts. I did not understand everything they said, but I felt their hatred and contempt. Forgotten kinships had been wakened by Ahearn's story, and I was stricken by grief and longing for what was gone.

Camelin did not return to the hearth, or join the men in their scornful talk. He stayed by Nolwynn and me. For that, and for what he told me, I have always loved him.

I never lost my yearning for the wolves. Though I had no clear memory of them, impressions came to me sometimes in that elusive place between reality and dreams. I saw fleeting images of a forest at night, a stretch of trampled earth, the deep hole of a wolf's den. There was warm fur and a great calm strength. I recalled the sound of breathing, and homely growls. The smell of milk enveloped me. There were images of rolling in the snow with a huge black wolf, and the mingled feelings of comfort and cold. I remembered the scent of trees and summer earth, and the power of walking with the wolves.

2

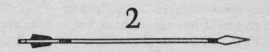

Thirteen summers have rolled across the land since Ahearn brought me to his clan. The time has not been easy for me. Against the suspicion and mockery of his people I have clawed out for myself a place of rough respect – not truly an adopted daughter's place, but a place higher than a slave's. As a sign that I am of the house of Ahearn, I wear about my head a scarlet leather band, and have his mark, an arrow, woven into the hem of my dress.

Nolwynn I love, for she is my one true friend and advocate. Ahearn I honour as the lord of the house in which I dwell, and as his clan's chieftain. Also I fear him because his word is life to me, or death.

His second wife, by whom he got three sons, taught me to play the lyre and to sing, for she saw some skill in me. She died last summer, fighting at his side in battle. He mourned her but briefly; always Nolwynn was his chief love. Now only Nolwynn, his three sons, and I live in Ahearn's house with him. His sons are younger than eleven summers, and too busy in their father's fields to concern themselves with me.

There is one more son, his eldest, born of Nolwynn before her accident. But he lives with another clan as pledge-son, given to keep the peace between our two villages. I cannot remember him, and he does not come to visit us. Ahearn never speaks of him, though Nolwynn says his name sometimes, in her dreams.

The clan calls me wolf-woman, and would have me for its slave if Nolwynn did not speak for me. As it is, I am busy enough in Ahearn's house, for it is my task to weave and make clothes for his family, and to grind grain for bread. And I must look after Nolwynn, for she can do nothing unaided save wash her face and hands and feed herself. Even those simple tasks are almost over-much, because her lungs are full of poisonous liquids and she slowly drowns. Sometimes I think the gods would have been kinder to let her drown quickly, that day in the river.

It is a morning early in my sixteenth summer, when Nolwynn's affliction so overwhelms her that she can hardly breathe, and I sing to her to ease her torment. After a while she is calm, and she puts her hand upon my arm. Her hand is narrow, and the veins on it are like blue cords. Her voice rasps in her throat.

"There is a heaviness in my heart," she says, "and I

8

fear for you when I am gone."

I am silent, sitting on the floor beside her sleeping-furs, for those same fears haunt me.

"I will this night speak with my lord," she says. "I will ask him to swear that when I am on my funeral pyre he will, in front of all the clan, vow that you are his adopted daughter. Instead of looking after me, you will work in the fields with his sons. The clan will not make you a slave, and your work will be honourable."

"I will be glad to do any work, wife of my lord," I say.

"Only three things will sever you from his protection," she says, and then she coughs awhile and cannot speak. I hold a bowl of water to her lips, but she shakes her head. She breathes as if wet rags are being held across her mouth.

"Three things," she whispers at last. I bend my head to hear her. "Your death. Crime, for if you break our laws you forfeit our hospitality. And marriage."

"The last is not likely," I say, smoothing her long pale hair back from her forehead. She is feverish, and her hair is wet. She coughs again, and her head falls back on the furs, for the talk has wearied her.

I sit stroking her hair, thinking that she sleeps. There is a small window-hole in the wall, and the sun streams warm upon her bed, its rays blue in the smoky haze. From outside come the distant sounds of women washing clothes in the lake, and children at play.

"It is quiet with the men gone," says Nolwynn, startling me. Her eyes remain closed, but her brows are drawn together in anxiety. She says, "I have dreams when they are away. I fear that one day my man will lose his fight, and it will be his head that is flaunted high on a wooden spike, on someone else's fence. They have been gone long, today."

"They have taken the youths with them," I remind her, "so they too can prove that they are warriors. They will not be back till dark, I think."

"Gibran was among the first-time warriors?" she asks.

"He surely went, but I did not notice him," I say, thinking how tall and excellent he had looked as he rode away with his great bow held proudly in his hand. The women did not go to fight today: this day was for the youths.

Nolwynn smiles faintly, and she opens her eyes a little and looks sideways at me. I lower my head. I am ashamed of my face, for the men of the clan call me a dark-head, and say I am ugly, with a wolf's eyes. The boys and girls mock me, throwing stones if they dare, though I have given them more bruises than they have given me. But in these past few seasons I have changed both outside and within. I do not fight any more, and when the young men taunt me I ache, and wish that I were beautiful. So when Nolwynn watches me closely now I hide my face behind my hair, and close my wolfish eyes.

She sighs. "You may be of a dark-haired clan, and an outcast," she says quietly, "but I know one youth who looks on you with favour."

"Your medicines have given you strange visions," I say, tidying her furs. Then I get up and go over to the house entrance. I push aside the skins covering the opening, and look out.

Ahearn's home, being the chieftain's dwelling, is the first of our few buildings. There are five houses, a

10

shelter for the animals, and a storehouse for our grain. The houses are low and circular, and the thatched roofs hang far beyond the walls with their open window-spaces. A flattened piece of ground stretches down to the moat that surrounds our place. This inner side of the moat is edged by a wooden fence made of spikes driven into the ground, and on the spikes are the skulls and decaying heads of defeated enemies. I try not to look at them, for the hair that remains on them is dark.

Through the wide gateway I see the moat, muddy and low in the summer heat. On the shores are canoes made from the hollowed trunks of trees. Most of them are on the far side, hidden in the long grass, waiting for the warriors when they return. Beyond rise the first tall trees of the forest, and to the right of the trees are the marshes, brown and tranquil and treacherous. Across the marshes is a path of reeds, stones, and branches that we have laid down to make a safe way to the clean waters. I see women walking back along that path now, carrying baskets of washing. When they reach the ground outside the moat they spread the washed linen and the woollen tunics on the grass to dry, and tell the children to lay them flat again should the wind tumble them. Then, talking and joking among themselves, they get into their canoes and paddle back across the moat to our village. I envy them their happy fellowship.

I turn again to the dark room, and look across to the fire. Nolwynn sleeps, freed for a time from her ordeals. I pile more wood on the fire, and replenish the firewood from the stack of branches outside. Taking a leafy branch from a corner, I sweep up and burn the old straw and the food scraps that litter the earthen floor, and strew about fresh dried grass with sweet-smelling herbs in it. I tidy the cups and bowls and knives on the wooden plank that serves for a table. There is no other furniture save a few low stools, a loom, and the worn fur rugs around the fire.

During the victory-feast tonight the entire village will be gathered here, sitting on these furs. They will drink ale, feast, tell stories, wrestle, and dance their frenzied dances; and maybe, towards morning, worn out from battle and celebration, they will ask me to sing for them.

And as I sing I will see the youth Gibran watching me ...

3

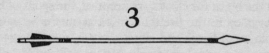

The celebration is boisterous tonight. The youths, having proved at last that they are men, leap up constantly during the feast and re-enact their killings. They shout with excitement, stamping in the scattered ashes of the fire, and sometimes on the plates of meat, their faces flushed and victorious. Their stories become confused, and arguments break out, to be settled with swords. Sometimes the fights are intense, and the children shrink back, enthralled and fearful. The old, hardened warriors chuckle at the younger ones, but their lined and scarred faces are full of pride. Wounded men, laughing at the antics of their companions, wait for the ale to dull their pain.

The fire spits and roars, its light leaping on the faces of the men and on their swords and furs and golden hair. It glistens on meat juices running down bearded chins, and shines in eyes ablaze with victory. Fur cloaks and woollen tunics, stained with sweat and blood, steam in the heat.

I take a portion of roasted pork and jostle through the turmoil to a place next to Nolwynn's bed. The men are sitting down again, still roaring about their conquests, and unwrapping the bundles they brought back with them from the fighting. The women and children press closer, eager to see what treasures will be theirs. There is a sudden hush.

As the black fur cloaks are unrolled, the spoils of battle lie revealed in the firelight: linen garments woven fine in colours of flame and cloud and sea; metal dishes and goblets, and priceless jewels; knives and swords, silver-hilted, glinting with precious stones; and finely wrought metal bracelets and brooches. It is a bounty finer than any they have won before.

For a while no one speaks. Then one of the women reaches across a fur and picks up a jewelled comb.

"What village did you plunder, for this?" she asks.

Ahearn leans forward, his hands toying with a cup of pure gold. "We found a king visiting one of his outlying villages," he says. "He had gone to persuade the men to fight for him against the invaders on his eastern border. He was guarded heavily, and had taken these for bribery. He fought well to keep them."

"So we battle kings now," says a younger woman, gravely. Her name is Morag. Her eyes, an unusual violet colour, are full of apprehension. "Be wary, lord. The

14

minor kings may band together against you, if you taunt them over-much. We cannot fight an army."

Ahearn strokes his beard. His hands are still stained with blood. His red woollen tunic, short to his knees, is patterned in black arrows along the hem and sleeves; his leather belt is carved with fine interlacing designs, and the silver clasp is jewelled. His tawny hair curls to his shoulders, and a long black fur cloak is fastened at his throat with a gold pin. He has not changed much since my earliest memory of him: he is still fair and fine, his face gentle one moment and full of killing rage the next. He is a good leader for his clan; his people seldom question him. In her mild cautioning, Morag risks his ire.

"I am always wary, woman," he says quietly. "And I choose my enemies – they do not choose me. Besides, kings dwell in towns safe behind stone forts, and the only paths they know are the roads they have trampled through their lands. They know not of our secret forest ways, or of our hidden sites. They may be the lordly stags, but we are the cunning wolves. Fear not." He picks up the golden cup and hands it to her. "It is fairly won by the blood of your kinsmen," he says. "Take it as my gift."

Morag flushes, and as she takes the cup his fingers touch hers, and hold. There is quiet chuckling from some of the men, and Ahearn, grinning, swears at them. Then he picks up a bronze spoon carved in complex patterns and set with rubies, and tosses it across the room to me. He alone gives me gifts, because I am of his household. Booty is shared only with a man's own family, unless he wishes to show another woman that he favours her. Unions are made and broken on the winnings of war.

Amid clamour and rejoicing, the other treasures are handed out. To sons are given the swords and knives; to wives and lovers the garments and the goblets and the jewels. Ahearn crosses the room, kneels by Nolwynn's bed, and gives her a silver brooch and a kiss. She is exhausted, fighting for each breath, but she smiles at him. For a while he strokes her head, his huge hands gentle in her hair and on her face, then he returns to the feast.

Towards the end of the gift-giving someone discovers, hidden in the folds of dark fur, a bundle of human hair, long and black and lustrous. One of the younger men claims it.

"I got it to remember her by," he says, choking on his ale, and wiping his mouth on his sleeve. "She fought me like a wildcat. But it is beautiful hair, is it not? It can be woven into a new tunic for me, in the shape of a black bird."

The hair is secured at one end by a cord. He flings it into the air, and for a while the men toss it about, making ribald remarks. Then one of them throws it at me. It lands on my feet, and I back away from it. He strides over, picks up the gleaming mane, and waves it in my face.

"It is black like yours, Tanith," he says. "Do you think it was from your clan? Do not turn away – she may have been your kinswoman! Sniff it – does it stink like your people?"

Pressing against the cold stone wall, I hide my face in my arms and scream at the man to let me be. He laughs and grabs my hair, wrapping it about his fist and pulling until my scalp aches.

"There is more here, for the weaving!" he cries. I hear a sword slide from its scabbard, and Nolwynn cries out, coughing and trying to speak.

Then comes Ahearn's voice, roaring and amused: "Is that what fighting men have come to – plundering girls' hair? Stay your blade, come back to the fire." He adds, with gentleness: "She is my wife's adopted daughter. Let her be."

Released, I swear quietly at the men's backs. Ahearn throws the hair on the fire, where it curls and melts. The atmosphere is tense, for some of the warriors resent Ahearn spoiling their entertainment and are tempted to challenge him to a sword fight – just to show that they are offended, and to impress their women. I wish they would fight, and my lord would give them a telling cut or two. But Ahearn glowers at them so fiercely that they forget their swords and get on with the feasting.

I sit close to Nolwynn's furs, my back against the wall, and refuse to eat again. Nolwynn rests, her face white as death. Even above the noise of the celebration, I can hear her breath rattling in her throat. I feel a cold wind blow in from the window-hole, and stand up to draw the heavy woven curtain. As I do so, I see the moon, full and round, rolling through the clouds. It overpowers me with longings. The moon in its fullness has always had this power over me, leaving me sleepless and hungering. It is hard to draw the curtain over its glory, its peace.

When all the gifts are given the men settle down, pile more branches on the fire, and pour more ale. It is then that Gibran stands. He holds in his arms something dark and loosely rolled, and he is looking at me.

"I brought a gift for you," he says. In front of them all he comes over and drops the bundle at my feet. He is smiling a little, embarrassed. By this act the whole clan will know he favours me. "It is not anything fine that men have made," he says, very low. "This is something else – a thing I killed in the forest, on the way back from the battle."

Speechless, I stand to acknowledge him. His face is in shadow, but I see the glimmer of his teeth and eyes. His hair blazes gold from the fire behind him. Flame-light glows in the fur of his cloak, and in the folds of his blue tunic.

I drop my gaze, and stoop to pick up the gift he has given me. It is a pelt, still damp on the skin side, and heavy. The animal was large, grey and brown like trees, and soft. I stand upright as I unroll it. Before me, smelling still of grass and sun-warmed earth, is the pelt of a wolf.

I hold it to my face, feeling the coarse hairs along the spine stiff against the softer fur beneath. Then I lift my head, and Gibran sees that my eyes are wet.

"I thought it would please you," he says gruffly. "I thought, because you once lived with them ..."

I cannot speak, and after a few moments he turns back to the fire, sits on the floor, and picks up his cup. He does not look at me again.

For a long time I stand with Gibran's gift in my hands, dimly aware of the feasting and drinking, and the music as the clan gets up to dance. Feet stamp, cloaks swirl, and the dust and smoke fly; yet I am mindful only of the wild warm odour of a wolf. Longing sweeps through me like a pain.

Later, when the celebrations are done, Ahearn hands me my lyre and tells me to sing. This night my songs are about the seasons of the earth, about the trees changing and the birds flying to warmer homes. But Gibran does not hear me sing; he has gone outside. When I have finished, the men fill their cups with ale again, and tell jokes.

I curl into my sleeping-furs, my face against the soft grey pelt. As I lie there I hear wolves howling far into the night; and in my dreams I think that they are calling me, and that one day I will go to them.

4

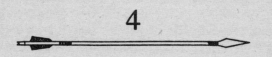

I raise my head, blink at the morning sun streaming
through the window-spaces, and look across the dirt floor
at the sleeping clan. They sprawl where they collapsed
the night before, some enveloped in cloaks, some curled
into furs, several of them still clutching their drinking-
cups. Ahearn lies in his sleeping-furs, his arms about
Morag's naked shoulders. Children nestle next to their
mothers, wrapped against the morning chill·in their long
skirts; and some of the younger women, made bold by
the night's revelry, have chosen their favourite young
warriors and lie with their arms around their necks.

Two have chosen Gibran, though I saw last night
that by the time they came to him he was beyond

noticing. He lies on his back, arms flung wide, with his head across the waist of the woman named Sabra. He looks boyish and vulnerable in sleep, his hair red-gold against the green of her garment.

Gibran belongs to another village, half a day's walk from here. His people are of the same race as Ahearn's clan, yet these fair-headed ones fight each other too, if they have the slightest cause. So the chieftains of both villages made a peace pact, since they must share the same forest for hunting and for gathering berries and plants; and they exchanged sons from their chieftains' houses, to secure the pledge. Ahearn's firstborn went to the other village, and Gibran was the son given in return. He has lived with Ahearn's people since he was five summers old, but he often visits his own clan, taking gifts for his father and bringing back gifts for Ahearn. He does not live in Ahearn's house, since Nolwynn needs quiet; he lives with a foster family in the house next to ours. He has high standing here because he is the son of the pledge. That he favoured me at the feast last night surprised me, but it must have astounded the clan. I know not why he did it, or what it is in me that he admires. Perhaps, like me, he feels solitary here.

I smile to myself and doze again, hugging the wolf pelt, and dream bold dreams.

The sound of Nolwynn coughing wakes me. I get up and go to her. "Would you like a drink?" I ask, lifting her shoulders to ease her breathing.

"No." She shakes her head, and coughs again. "Why so much smoke? The air is thick."

"The fire is almost out, wife of my lord. The air is

clean, save for the stench of ale and warriors. We will fill the bathing-tubs today, and make them soak themselves. And their clothes."

Nolwynn coughs, chokes, and swallows noisily. She draws her breath in terrible gasps, and I see that her lips are blue.

"I will revive the fire and heat water, and the steam will help you breathe," I say, laying her down again. "And when you are comfortable, I will sing to you."

Nolwynn shakes her head and grasps my hand. "I heard – I heard your kinsfolk calling for you – in the night," she says hoarsely.

"My kinsfolk? Your enemies?"

"No." She closes her eyes against her pain, fights to speak. "Not our enemies. Your kin. They – " She coughs again, and I move to go to the firepit. Her fingers tighten on my wrist, but her grip is weaker than a child's. I bend my head close to her lips. Her voice is no more than the wind whispering in the reeds.

"I heard them howling," she says. "Did you hear?"

"I heard them," I reply.

"Perhaps it is time for you to – " She chokes, and cannot speak. I stand and go to throw more kindling wood on the embers. Quickly I fill a shallow metal bowl with water, and place it in the hot ashes.

When I return to Nolwynn she is lying motionless, her eyes open and gazing at the shaft of morning light above her sleeping place. She is dead.

5

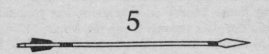

"I will bear you sons and daughters of your own," says Morag, as she places on Ahearn's table her clay bowls and cooking things, and the golden cup. "I do not wish to have an adopted daughter. She goes, my lord."

I stare at Ahearn, willing him to speak for me, but he continues slowly to clean the small pelt of a fox that he has spread across his knees. His eyes are sad. I gaze out the window-hole above the empty place where for many long seasons Nolwynn has lain. Outside, her funeral pyre still burns. There have been no promises.

The only sounds are the crackling of the fire and the slow scraping of the chieftain's knife as he cleans the flesh from the pelt. At last I speak.

"My lord, I have no wish to leave your household. Let me stay and I will be of use to both of you. I will weave your garments, bake your bread, help in your fields, and when the sons are born I will help care for – "

"My sons will not be touched by a dark-head!" hisses the new woman. "Nothing of mine will be touched by you! I will not – "

"Silence!" roars Ahearn, leaping up, and flinging the pelt on the floor. He shakes his knife in Morag's face, the point barely missing her nose. "I will not have women squawking like hens in my presence! *I* am lord in this house! *I* choose who will come and who will go! One night's pleasuring does not win for you the right to rule my house, Morag. So keep silent, lest your tongue lose you the place the rest of you has won."

He lowers his knife, and faces me. For a while he is silent, breathing deeply, his eyes like ice. At last he says: "You, adopted daughter of my once-wife ... You stay, but if you fight again with this new woman, you will go. You are no more an adopted daughter."

"Then what am I, lord?" I ask, afraid.

"Whatever Morag calls you," he says, and goes out.

Morag continues to place her things on the wooden table. One by one she picks up the cups and bowls that were Nolwynn's, and smashes them on the hearth. With her foot she pushes the broken pieces into the embers. Finally she turns and looks at me. Her red lips curve, but her face is cold.

"I desire to cook a special thing for my lord tonight, to comfort him," Morag says. "I desire to cook him fish. Go to the fishing place on the far side of the lake, and catch three for me."

24

"New wife of my lord, it is late in the day already, and the fishing place is a long walk from here. It will be dark when I come back through the forest, and dangerous. Tomorrow I – "

"Do it," she says. "Do not come back till you have caught them."

"I do not have to do this. Even the men will not walk outside our village at night."

"You must do everything you are commanded," says Morag harshly. "You are no more an adopted daughter, says my lord. You are what I say you are."

"A fisherwoman?" I cry. "Is that what I am now – a hunter for whatever food you have a hunger for?"

"Oh, not a hunter," replies Morag, with a slow smile. "You are not as prized as a hunter. Now get bait and go, else it will be night before you start. And Tanith, remember – if you are lost in the mire, you are on your own. Our men will not waste their time or their strength looking for a slave."

* * *

The day is far gone when I lower the baited bronze hook into the fishing-hole. I sit back on the grassy bank and wait, looking across the still blue waters edged with the subtle brown of the vast marshlands. We have a track through the marshes to this fishing place, but at night the track cannot be seen and the bog is perilous. Beyond the waters thin columns of smoke from our village rise straight into the evening air.

Along the shore from me is a stretch of grass sloping down from the forest. The shadows are dark between the trees. I shiver and put my hand on the knife I carry at my waist, though it will be small use against bears or wildcats. I lean closer to the water, the line held firmly in my hand, and start singing quietly. It is a song of woman-power and fire, and by it I defy the spirits of the gathering dark.

The line jerks, pulls taut; and after a short, fierce fight I pull in a small salmon. I drop the hook again, and am about to continue my song when there is a movement in the grass further along the shore. I am still, and very quiet.

A wolf cub comes down to the lake, drinks thirstily, and starts to walk back up again. He is bowled over by another cub, a female, and they roll together on the sandy soil, snapping and yelping in play. They are not yet half-grown. Their fur is dark and soft, their bellies are fat, their legs ungainly, with paws too big for them. A she-wolf arrives and stares at them a moment as if she is tempted to join them, and then she too goes to the water to drink. She is magnificent, full of strength and gracefulness. They are but five long strides away from me.

A bee settles on my hand, and I move just one finger to brush it off. The she-wolf looks up, directly at me. She stands in the last brilliant rays of the sun, and every hair and whisker is alive with light. Her eyes are translucent amber jewels, and the velvet fur is coppery on her upper nose and around her eyes. The sides of her nose, and her throat, are white as milk. The rest of her is brown and grey, and shining.

Enthralled, I dare not move. The wolf stares back, her gaze unblinking. She seems at ease, curious and observant.

"My kinswoman, you are beautiful," I say.

One of the cubs makes a daring run towards me, tail wagging madly, then changes his mind, skids to a halt, somersaults backwards, and flees to his mother. He nips her tail and her hind legs, baiting her for a game, but she turns and snarls at him. The cub cringes, nose low on the dirt between his paws, ears laid back against his head. The she-wolf ignores him, and looks back at me.

The line tugs in my hands. It is another salmon, larger than the first. I look at the she-wolf again. Her ears are pricked forward and her black lips part in a wolfish smile. Still there seems nothing violent about her, only a calm inquisitiveness.

I haul in the fish, keeping a watch on the she-wolf. The other cub trots towards me along the shore, stopping only two strides away. She is dark brown with bands of paler brown about her neck. Her eyes too are amber, bright and beautiful. She bares her teeth at me.

"Is it a fish you want?" I say, throwing her the smaller one. It flaps on the dirt between her forepaws, and she leaps straight up into the air, alarmed. Then she starts prancing around the fish, pawing at it and sniffing. Every time the fish moves the cub leaps, pretending fright, and soon her brother comes over to play as well. The she-wolf moves closer.

The cubs play with the fish until the female realises it is edible and swallows it, and then they sidle up to me, daring each other to steal the second one. They do not stare directly into my eyes, as their mother does; they look at me sideways, their tails wagging. I long to throw them the larger fish, but I dare not, for it is Morag's.

The she-wolf watches, all the time coming closer.

After a while the cubs run off along the bank, splashing in the shallows. The she-wolf stays, staring and alert. Her eyes, no longer lit by the sun, are deep as yellow pools. She makes no sound, just looks at me. I move my hand a little, to touch her; she moves back, warily. Slowly, slowly I move, until my hand is outstretched towards her. She leans forward, sniffs my fingers. Her muzzle is soft, her whiskers tickle, her breath is quick and warm. She licks my hand; I am singing inside, for joy. Then she turns aside, sniffs the grass about my fishing place, and gulps down the salmon that is Morag's. She examines the line and hook, then moves to go.

I stand up, longing for her to stay. "You were mother and father to me," I say.

The she-wolf turns again, her head dark now in the twilight. Her breath steams in the cool air, and tiny insects dance above her. She smells of earth and summer wind.

With the strangest feelings tearing at my heart, I watch as she and her cubs go away. Then I fish again, but catch nothing this time for Morag. I fear her anger, but I fear more being alone in the night. I pick up the hook and line, unsheath my knife, and begin the long walk back along the forest ways to a place that is no longer home.

6

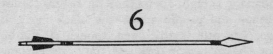

This is the first time, since I have lived with Ahearn's clan, that I have been in the forest after twilight. I know my path, for I have walked this way a thousand times, gathering wild apples, marjoram, eggs, and whortle-berries. But at night it is another world. I realise, with surprise, that I am not afraid. I feel complete, as if something strong in me is restored. Perhaps this is how I felt in my forgotten life, when I walked through the night with the wolves.

The darkness enfolds me, the trees are sentinels, and the moon is my lamp. It does not make me yearn tonight, this moon; tonight I am free in its silver beams, and there is rapture in me.

I hear the grunts of animals, the screeches of night birds, and rustlings in the undergrowth. I see no living thing save plants, but I am watched. I feel no danger here. It is as if the night breathes and the earth breathes with it, and life and death ebb and flow in harmony. Somewhere nearby an owl swoops, and a rat squeals. Fur and flesh become wings, and fly. I think of Nolwynn on the funeral pyre, becoming smoke and sky, and I mourn.

There are eyes at my back, following me. I spin about quickly, glimpse a shadow melting into the dark. I hear no sound and do not see the wolf, but I feel her presence guarding me.

The moon is high when I drop the fishing things into my canoe and paddle across the black moat to the village. The gate is still open, though all the houses except Ahearn's are in darkness, their fires burning low while their occupants sleep. But Ahearn's fire blazes, and Morag sits alone beside it. Ahearn's sons are all asleep, curled into their straw and furs against the firelit walls. Morag's face is buried in her hands, and a bowl of stew sits on the hearth, keeping warm. For me? Then I notice that Ahearn's hunting bow is gone, and his bearskin boots.

"Where is my lord?" I ask.

Morag leaps up, calling out in shock.

"You have come back!" she cries.

"I hope I have," I say, "else I am a ghost, and my real self lies back there in the bellies of the wolves, with the fishes I had caught for you."

For a while Morag is speechless, her face red in the firelight, and full of dismay. I cannot understand why.

"Why has my lord gone hunting at this hour?" I ask, picking up the bowl of stew, and dipping my fingers into it. I am hungry.

She grabs it from me.

"He is not hunting, fool!" she cries. "He is out searching for you! He cursed half the men in the clan, because they would not go with him! You have caused trouble in our camp. For the first time men have opposed Ahearn. He was so angry when he went."

"But he knows I would not walk across the marshes in the dark," I say. "He knows I would come back on the forest path. How is it that we missed each other?"

Morag's face flushes deeper, and she sits down and carefully wipes her finger across the stew that trickles down the outside of the bowl. She will not look at me.

"You did not tell him where I was," I say, very quiet. "You lied to him. You told me to go to the fishing place when it was so late I could not safely return before the night – and you hoped I would never come back. Then you lied, said I'd run away. The men would not look for a slave, you said. Well, one did. The gods help you when he finds out that you knew all the time where I was."

"He'll not find out," says she, coldly. "You have no claim on him, wolf-woman – he'll listen to you no more. But I – I am his comfort now, and all his happiness. He'll not turn aside from me. He'll hold to everything I say."

"You do not know him," I say.

"Better than you know him," she says. "You know nothing, wolf-woman. Nolwynn protected you. You were not there when we had our clan meetings. Many

31

times they would have cast you out, but she defied them, and Ahearn was swayed by her words because she was his wife. But now he is all mine. And I'll not speak for you, nor plead on your behalf. You are alone. And you will be worse than alone, if he dies out there in the wilds while he looks for you. For by the gods, Tanith, I swear that I shall punish you."

I go over to my sleeping place, roll out my furs, and crawl between them. I can hear Ahearn's youngest son sniffing in his dreams, or perhaps he cries. He loves his father. His name is Liam, and he is eight summers old. To comfort him I sing, very softly.

"Your singing will not sweeten your position here now," mocks Morag, placing the stew in the embers to heat for when her lord returns. "I have no pain that you can ease. You are useless to me."

"I do not sing for you," I reply. "I sing for myself."

"Better to weep," she says.

For as long as it takes for the moon to sail across the sky, we are silent. Then Ahearn comes home. We hear him shuffling and grunting outside the door, then the heavy skins are swept aside and in he comes with a gust of cold dawn wind, limping and cursing, and leaning on a sturdy branch. His right boot is black with blood.

"I found her not," he says, stumbling to the fire, and sinking down beside Morag. His face is grey and shines with sweat, and he breathes in heavy gasps.

"I was followed by a bear," he says hoarsely. "I wounded it, then fell down a rocky bank while I fled."

Morag kneels before him and draws off his fur-lined boot. He swears in agony. His foot is drenched with blood, and unnaturally twisted. By the fire's glow I see splintered bones protruding from the bruised and torn flesh.

Ahearn takes one look, and curses foully. "By the gods, 'tis not a marching-hoof for a warrior!" he cries. "Go and get Hrothi. And bring me ale, lots of it."

Morag sees me standing in the shadows at Ahearn's back.

"I shall wake our healer, lord," she says, and flees.

Ahearn sits grimly contemplating his injured foot. I walk around him until I am almost in front of him. He has covered his face with his hands, and is groaning with pain.

"I can mix you herbal medicines, lord," I say.

His head jerks up. His eyes are terrible.

"Hrothi told me his secrets, so that I could help Nolwynn ..." My voice trails off, and I stare in fear at his face.

"By the gods, girl! Where did you spring from?" he yells.

"I have been here all the time, lord. Your new wife demanded that I catch some fish for her, though the day was far gone. It took me until dark to catch them. Then I walked home again through the forest, along our path."

"So you were here, safe in your sleeping-furs, while I was out searching?"

"Yes, lord. Your new wife knew where I was. She – "

"Do you know what calamity you have caused? You have destroyed my rank as chieftain! Because of you I can no longer hunt or fight, or lead my men to battle! Because of you this thing has come to pass, that leaves me crippled and no more a warrior! You do well to stand away from me, wolf-woman. I would break your neck for this!"

"I told you, lord, I was fishing. Your new wife – "

"Speak not of her! I lay all this on you, Tanith. I curse the day I saw your sea-green eyes and stuffed you in my saddlebag! Fool, fool I am, to ever think that you could stand in the place of my daughter. You have brought me the greatest grief, the worst catastrophe that could befall a fighting man. I had rather my head were on a victor's spike than stumble about for the rest of my life like a drunken clod."

"It will only be for the span of a few full moons, my lord. Men have had broken feet before, and walked."

"Walked, yes! But stood and fought like champions, no! Oh, Tanith, you do not know what you have done to me!"

"I have done nothing, lord, except do as I was – "

"Keep silence! Your very voice bedevils me. Go! Get out of my house!"

Fleeing, I am confronted at the door by Hrothi, his instruments of surgery wrapped up in a bloodstained hide. Morag is behind him, with Tallil, the clan's priest, and four men to hold the chieftain down. Smiling a little, Morag glances at me, and I turn and run away.

I get in my small canoe, throw the ill-fated fishing things into one of the other boats, and paddle across to the forest side. When I have dragged the canoe into the grasses, I sit under the trees, looking back at the village.

The houses crouch in the dawn, and smoke from newly kindled fires rises from gaps in the thatched roofs. Behind the village lie our fields of wheat, ripening to gold. After one more full moon it will be time for the harvest, time for joyful work in the hot summer days, and feasting through the nights. But now the fields wait in silence, and the air is cool. I shiver and wrap my arms about my legs. My summer shift is woven finer than my winter robes, and my arms are bare. I wish I had brought a cloak.

Suddenly a man screams. Again and again he screams, and I hear Hrothi yelling at his aides to hold him.

I get up and run further into the forest. I run until I can no longer hear Ahearn's agony, and then I rest against a tree, breathing painfully, my mind in turmoil.

7

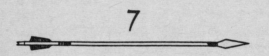

Over and over I think on the happenings of this night, struggling to understand them. Out of all the confusion and grief, one thing stands clear, and torments me. Ahearn commanded me to leave his house: is this banishment? I do not know, and the uncertainty is worse than the command itself.

At last I wipe my face on my hands and start walking. I do not care where I am going, and though I know well the clan's pathways through the forest, I do not keep to them. The sun begins to sparkle through the pines, the air becomes warm. A breeze blowing against my face carries sounds of yelping and growling. Thinking of the wolf cubs I saw yesterday, I move into the shade of the trees, and creep forward.

In a small clearing I see them. The cubs are cavorting in a patch of sunlight, rolling and jumping onto their mother, who is stretched out on the ground, trying to sleep. Nearby, his dark pelt gleaming, lies a huge male. A smaller male, paler in colour, sits under a tree washing himself. They all have bulging sides, telling of a good night's hunt, and now they are relaxing in the morning sun. I shrink against a tree, unmoving, hardly daring to breathe. The wind blows towards me, and though I can smell the wolves, they cannot smell me.

The cubs become more frenzied in their attempts to goad their mother into a game. They tear at her ears with their teeth, bite her hindquarters, and leap on her so heavily that her body shakes. She tolerates them for a long time, then raises her head and growls. They cower back, whimpering, and for a moment or two give her peace. But as soon as she puts down her head and closes her eyes, they are on her again, biting her tail hard enough to make her yelp. She leaps up and nips at them. They run off, and she sits licking the small wounds they have given her. The cubs creep close again, plotting an ambush.

The smaller male has finished his wash, and is watching the cubs. Suddenly he bounds towards them, frightening them so much that they leap into the air, tails bristling. Softly he growls and then runs a little distance away, watching them sideways, daring them to follow. They do. He endures their torments with patience that amazes me, but sometimes they get too vicious, and he snarls at them in earnest. They cringe before him, bellies on the ground, tails tucked between their legs. Their fluffy ears lie flat against their heads, their narrowed eyes do not dare to meet his. He stands over them, growling, then walks away with his tail erect and his legs stiff, as if he no longer condescends to know them. They watch him go, their eyes bright; then they launch themselves at him in another onslaught, and they all tumble and snap and snarl until the dust flies.

The big wolf gets up and goes over to the she-wolf. Gently he mouths her ears and snout, and she whines and rolls on her back, caressing his face and neck with her huge paws. They are tender together, whining softly and nuzzling one another. I realise that he is her mate, and the father of the cubs. Then he sits beside her, tail wagging, grinning so hideously and happily that I laugh. Immediately he sees me, and I freeze. His grin vanishes. His ears prick forward, and his black lips close. Slowly he stands, his burning eyes on my face. The other wolf stops his play with the cubs, and also confronts me. The cubs, sensing the tension, are still, and in an instant the she-wolf too is on her feet, head turned to me.

I do not move. The big male runs towards me a little way, sniffing, then stops. He is a massive beast, almost as high as my waist, and longer than a man is tall. His ears move back, and he thrusts his great head forward. His body is stiff and aggressive. He pulls back his lips in a warning snarl, exposing his teeth. His growl is a savage rumble coming from the depths of him, from the core of the ancient earth itself.

He steps towards me, then stops, all his body telling his fury. I anger him, but I do not know why; and, as if sensing my inexperience, he halts his attack. I am afraid, not of him but of myself, because he is communing with me and I do not understand, and my ignorance could be fatal. I am in awe of him. His presence overwhelms me, seems to fill the forest and blot out the sun.

In some far part of my mind is a voice screaming at me to run; in another quieter part is the awareness that to run would mean certain death. It takes me all my strength just to stand and look into his eyes. And then I realise: it is by staring that I challenge him. So I do what the cubs do, when they appeal for tolerance. I kneel on the ground in front of him, my eyes narrowed and turned aside, my face against the earth. The growling changes, becomes low and soft. I feel the wolf come close, hear his massive paws shifting in the dust.

A hundred seasons I wait. All my life hangs in his power, swinging between his wildness and his restraint. I know that if he were a man and I his enemy, I would be slain by now without mercy. But I still live and, though the wolf growls, I feel no hate in him.

"I trust you with my life, kinsman," I say. "I have no argument with you."

The wolf stops growling. I feel his breath on the back of my neck, and he sniffs my wrists and hands. I have no fear, only a sense of wonder, and deep respect. Bygone memories flash across my mind: a hole in the ground; the remains of a rabbit; and a wolf, close, like this.

Without raising my eyes I stroke the wolf's chest and the pale fur of his chin. He takes my hand in his mouth and chews it gently. He does not hurt. I dare to look up, and see his eyes near to mine, brilliant and overpowering. I cannot look at them for long. He lets go my hand, and we sit together. Peace washes over me. I feel as if he knows everything about me, and accepts me utterly. There is no judgement, no prejudice. I feel cleansed. And when the wolf leans his head against mine, I weep for sheer joy, and know I have at last come home.

When he stretches out to sleep, I lie just beyond his shadow. The sun is on my face, and my kinsfolk lie about me, dozing in the summer heat. I open my eyes a slit, and look at them.

The she-wolf watches me, her nose upon her paws, but she is easy. The other male rests in the shade, and every now and again he opens one eye and looks at the cubs. Exhausted at last, they sprawl on their backs with their round bellies exposed to the sun, legs splayed. Compared with their noble elders they are ruffianly and ridiculous, and I love them.

I sing them all a song, a song of happiness and home-coming, and their ears move as they listen. Then I lie in silence, and think of names for them.

The cubs are easy. I call the male Zaal and his sister Zeki, which are our old clan words for trouble and trickery. The she-wolf I call Shula, which means bright-ness, because I love her eyes. The younger male is Kalasin, because he is the keeper of the little ones. And the chief wolf, the one to whom I entrusted my life, I call a name that means blessing-giver. I call him Ashok.

8

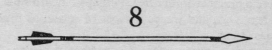

When it is dark I return to Ahearn's house. He lies on his straw bed close to the fire, and Morag is weaving. The colours on her loom are black and scarlet. Her hands do not stop when I come in, nor does she look up. His two older sons recline on a fur a small distance away, playing a game with clay dice. Liam sits alone, unhappily, hugging a small leather horse his father made him. Only Liam acknowledges me, glancing at me briefly, and smiling.

I kneel at my lord's side and wait for him to turn his head. I know he does not sleep, for though his eyes are closed his eyelids flicker, and his breathing is uneven.

"My lord, there is something I am not sure about,"

I say. "Am I to stay, or go?"

For a long time he says nothing. My legs go numb beneath me, but I wait. At last he says: "Stay and sing, Tanith."

And so I sing for him, as I often sang for Nolwynn, to fly his mind above his pain and bring him peace. It is a song she loved, an ancient song of a goshawk soaring near the sun, and while I sing Ahearn turns his head away and puts his hand across his eyes. He weeps very quietly, and I dare not move to comfort him, for tears are a sign of greatest weakness in a man. I too grieve, thinking of Nolwynn. Twice I sing the song, as I sang it always twice for her. She loved the freedom of it, while she lay a prisoner in her bed. Perhaps Ahearn now feels the same way, and weeps for loss of action as much as for loss of her.

I sing five more songs before Ahearn sleeps. Then I stand and inspect the cooking-pot for food, eagerly, for I have not eaten all day. But there is nothing left, so I go and sit on my sleeping-furs. I stroke the wolf pelt that Gibran gave me, but have no comfort from it. I think how once the wolf in it breathed and panted and bayed beneath the moon; how its heart beat and its eyes glowed like Shula's eyes. Perhaps it was mate to the lone Kalasin; perhaps it was Ashok's brother. Perhaps they mourn for this wolf, as I mourn for Nolwynn.

I wrap the pelt up tight and firm, and offer it to the god I love more than all of them: the one we call the Lion and the Lamb, because he is the bringer of kingship and the bringer of peace. He is a new god, given to our people by priests from across the sea. They told us to give up our ancient gods, because the new one is mightiest, but we keep the new god alongside our other ones, and worship whom we please. I revere the Lion and the Lamb because it is said he loves all living things and proclaims their harmony. So I dedicate the pelt to him, and then burn it on the fire.

Morag and the sons say nothing. But Morag notices the scratches on my hands and arms, where the cubs have played a little rough with me. She gives me a dark and knowing look, and soon afterwards leaves the house. I sit and watch the fire. The smoke from the pelt rises in a black column to our roof, and pours out through the smoke-hole into the night. I see it drifting dark against the stars, and think of wolves' eyes.

The pelt is ashes when Morag returns, Hrothi and Tallil with her. She gives the priest a stool to sit on, for he is a respected visitor. Hrothi pulls back the furs that cover Ahearn so that he can examine his foot. Ahearn wakes, and swears at him.

Hrothi has set Ahearn's broken foot in clay, binding it solidly with sticks and thick leather strips, and placing heated stones about it to set the clay. Now he replaces the stones with ones newly heated from the hearth. Then he prepares more drugged ale, and gives it to Ahearn. When all that can be done is done, Hrothi stands and gives Tallil a look full of meaning.

The priest, a tall, thin man in a long black robe, stands up. Sacred charms from our ancient gods hang from his hemp belt, and he wears a great jewelled cross about his neck. Tonight he carries a staff decorated with human bones. The priest is not old, but he has an imposing look about him, and his wisdom is celebrated. He has taught us that the earth is a garden the gods gave to us. Our life's work is to tend that garden, to grow crops and fruit, and look after the animals. In this way we will please the gods. Tallil also foretells the future, and knows the secret doors to the underworld. By his rituals he can discern which days the gods will favour the clan in battle, and which days they will not. Ahearn makes no important move without his blessing, and on the night of every new moon, accompanied by the priest, he sacrifices one of his precious goats to appease the gods. He holds Tallil's word as final law.

With all the clan, I honour the priest. But there is something veiled about him that I do not trust. There is another power he has, an unearthly skill, that is not often shown to us. When he stands before me now, dark and tall against the firelight, I am afraid.

"Stand, Tanith," he says, his voice gentle.

I do as he commands, but I avoid his eyes. I look at the cross about his neck, for that is the sign of the god I love.

"Hold out your arms," he says, and I obey. He sees the scratches there, and slowly shakes his head. Then he brandishes the staff over me, making the bones rattle, and invokes the gods to protect us all. He drops the staff on the floor between us, and it rolls against my feet. I do not like the coldness of the bones against my skin, and step back. The staff rolls against my feet again. I do not move, for fear.

"The bones are the bones of truth," Tallil says. "If you try to deceive me, the bones will rattle out their protest, and you will be found out. Search your heart carefully, before you answer me. What are your beliefs, child?"

"I believe ... I believe that the greatest thing is

mercy, and that force is not always right. I believe in the Lion and the Lamb, that we are beloved of him, and that all life is holy."

The priest nods solemnly, a frown creasing his high forehead. "And this clan, Tanith. Think carefully. What think you of this clan?"

"There are some here I love, lord. Ahearn, and the ashes of his once-wife. I honour the pledge-son. I respect them all, because they sheltered me when Ahearn took me from the wolves."

"But you never stopped thinking of the wolves, did you, Tanith? You never stopped being their child. They have called you, entranced you. And now you have returned to them, and let them put their savage mark on you. Tell me the truth. Have you not always hated Ahearn for taking you from them?"

"No! That is not true!" In my distress I move a little, and the bones jostle and babble on my feet. I try to calm myself, to keep very still. "I do not hate anyone," I say. "Not a single one in this clan. It is they who despise me."

"They despise you? They despise you, who gave you shelter and food and clothing, and let you live defended and kept by them? You have a twisted heart, child. The people of this clan are noble and good. Their warriors are brave, and strong, and in favour with the gods."

"I do not believe that a warrior is strong because he kills a child, or that he is brave because he torments a woman. The wolves are more just than that."

"So, we come to it," says the priest. "The poison in you. Love for the savage, hate for the good."

"I told you, lord, I have no hate for anyone."

"Maybe so. But even your love is dangerous. You said you love Ahearn. But it is because of you that he was, last night, grievously wounded. What kind of love is this, Tanith? Love that wounds, that tears and breaks? I say it is a deadly love you have. A love fatally close to the wickedness of wolves."

"Wolves are not wicked, lord," I say. I keep still, so still, though my heart quakes.

Tallil's eyes narrow as he listens intently. The bones are quiet.

"That is only your word against the great truths in our stories and songs," he says. "Since time began the wolves have been known for their cunning and their evil ways. They have poisoned you, and you cannot see their wickedness. How many times have you been back to them?"

"Only once. Today."

"Then it may not be too late. They have called you once, and sliced their sign upon your flesh. If they call you again and you answer, they may carve their mark upon your spirit, then you will be forever lost. I warn you, Tanith: the wolves are bad, and full of guile. Before you know it, they will have you trapped. And then they will use you to bring harm to this clan, for that is the scheming way of wolves.

"Guard yourself against them. Take care of your spirit, guard it against the evil that deceives you. Kneel, child, and I shall pray for you."

I step over the staff, and kneel in front of him. But I do not hear Tallil's words as he guards my soul against the evils of the wild. I hear instead, with fierce joy, the sound of a wolf howling far away in the night.

When the prayer is finished and the priest lifts me to my feet, he sees that I am crying. I think he takes it as a sign that I am penitent, for he blesses me, and says no more about my dangerous love.

He picks up the staff and goes. When he has gone I glance at Morag. I know she has heard all that the priest has said, and that she stores it in her heart to use another day.

9

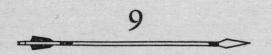

It rains. It has rained so many days that our moat is filling up and the ground about our houses is turned to mud. Every day the children take the canoes across to the other side, and gather up huge piles of grass to bring over to our goats, kept safe within the animal shelter. It is too stormy now to let them graze by the forest edge, with goatherds out there all day to guard them. Even the horses are restless, in their high enclosure beside the wheatfield. But there is exhilaration in the rain: yesterday the clan put out pots to catch the pure water, and played and danced naked in the downpour to wash themselves. I saw the youths wrestling one another for sport, and Gibran was among them. He was slender and strong, white and shining in the rain. I did not go out.

Ahearn is in great pain. He has a fever, and his leg above his foot is turning black. Hrothi comes and goes all day with his potions and his worried looks, and in the evenings Tallil stands beside the chieftain's bed and chants prayers. At night Morag slides beneath Ahearn's sleeping-furs with him, but he bellows at her if she disturbs his foot. By morning she is always in her own bed, and we are all weary from disturbed rest.

Hrothi is with Ahearn now, deciding with the priest what is to be done about the chieftain's injured foot. There is talk among the clan that they will cut the foot off, but I know that Ahearn would rather die than be forever crippled. The clan blames me for his catastrophe, and no one speaks to me. So I sit here in the rain by my canoe, on the moat side of the spiked fence so no one can see me. I am tempted to paddle across and visit the wolves. But they will be in their den, and I do not know where it is. Warm it would be, with them.

There is a movement beside me. It is Gibran, with rain like tears upon his face, and his gold hair streaming wet on the dark fur of his cloak. He wears a short tunic, brown as hazelnuts, and his legs and feet are bare. He crouches in the mud with me, places his spear across two stones, and folds his hands in front of him. His hands are strong, and beautiful. He is all beautiful.

He smiles, and I fly to pieces inside.

"I have it in my mind to go hunting," he says.

"What will you hunt?" I ask.

"Hares, maybe a fox." He hesitates, then says: "I will not hunt for wolves again."

I blush, knowing that he knows I burned the pelt.

"I am not angry, wolf-woman," he says, and on his lips the name is not a mockery. "I was at first, because I went to trouble to get that pelt for you. Then I thought how I would feel if someone gave me a gift of my brother's skin. I think I, too, would make a funeral pyre."

"Neither was I angry," I said. "I loved the pelt, and honour you for giving it to me."

"Why did you burn it, then?"

"Because I have living wolves to comfort me."

"Do you need comforting, Tanith?"

I look at him; his eyes are very grave. He is frowning a little, as if he cares what my answer is.

"Perhaps comfort is not the word," I say. "It is company. Acceptance. Kinship."

"And you have that with savage beasts?"

"Not with savage beasts," I say. "With the wolves."

"It is the same thing, Tanith."

"I think not, from my acquaintance with them."

"You are a strange woman."

"I am of an enemy clan. What else could you expect?"

"I do not know what I expect with you, Tanith. That is what beguiles me. Now, will you give me a blessing for the hunt, so I will be successful?"

"Tallil gives the blessings. According to him, I can only bring a curse."

"According to me, anyone who runs with wolves has courage and a hunter's heart. So I ask your blessing."

"I bless your hunting, then," I say. He smiles; his teeth are even and perfect, and when his lips are serious again, his eyes still smile. The rain is running into the hollows of his throat. He picks up his spear, then stands and hauls a canoe down to the moat. The rain hisses

50

on the water, and as he paddles across he is enveloped in mist.

Later, as I enter Ahearn's house, I pass Hrothi and Tallil on their way out. The healer gives me a look so filled with hatred that I shrink from him. I dare not look at the priest.

When they are gone Morag says: "They are coming back in a while, to cut off my lord's foot. See now what your evil has brought to us."

I look at Ahearn. He lies still, deadly white. An empty potion-cup is near his bed.

"It is your fault, not mine," I say to Morag, "because you lied to him when he went out to look for me."

She comes over to me and strikes me hard across the face. I do not hit her back because she is Ahearn's wife, and his sons are watching. I go outside again, the taste of blood salty in my mouth; and I hurt in my heart more than in my head where I was struck.

I sit in the mud on the moat's edge, rocking back and forth in my despair. The rain beats down and the skies thunder. I hear Ahearn screaming, and cover my ears with my hands.

After a long time there is silence. The rain has stopped, and I look up to see that it is almost dark. Across the swollen waters of the moat, just on the forest's edge, Ashok sits in the last daylight, keeping vigil over me.

I go back to Ahearn's house, feeling weary and weighted down with pain. As I push aside the skins in the doorway I look back. Ashok is gone. It is Gibran who watches me as he paddles towards me over the moat, a young deer across the bow of his canoe.

10

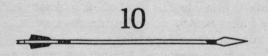

The night is warm, and the moist ground inside our house steams in the fire's heat. As I lie in my furs on the damp straw, I listen to Ahearn moan and sob in his sleep. I am dismayed; it is as if he is a child again, and not a man. I pull the furs over my head, but still I can hear his agony, and I cannot sleep for that and other miseries.

Outside, the waters drip off the edges of our roof, and tiny streams run down towards the moat. I hear the goats restless in their shelter. From deep in the forest comes the howl of a wolf.

I get out of my bed, put on a dry fur cloak, and bind on my leather boots. All the family sleeps, and no one sees me go.

In the forest, mist from the warm earth rises all around me. The air is cool, and I see stars above the roof of trees. It is very dark, but I do not care that I can no longer see my path. Far away I hear a wolf call, and another answers it. A madness comes upon me, and I, too, howl. A comic howl it is, a scratch upon the night against the swelling song of theirs. But I long to call to them, so I do what I do best – I sing.

While I sing, I walk deeper into the forest, beyond the paths I know, beyond the places where I gathered berries and where the marjoram grows. The forest is black and shadowy in front of me; the world behind me is darker still. Then I see amber eyes watching me from the way ahead. I stop a little distance away, not certain who it is, and crouch down low and avert my eyes. The wolf walks towards me, his lips open in a grin, his tail wagging. He turns side on, not looking straight at me, then walks back a short way from where he came, watching me over his shoulder. It is Kalasin.

"Are you come to lead me home?" I say, standing up again.

He lifts his nose and howls. It is a stirring sound, hollow and deep and echoing. When it has died I hear another howl from far away, in answer. I have the strangest feeling that the wolves speak to one another of me; that Kalasin says he has found me, and Ashok says that he knows. I am in awe of them, that they can commune across such a distance. And then another thought astounds me: they knew the moment I set foot into their territory, and Kalasin came to meet me, like an arrow through the night. Even more than that: I think, with wonder, that the wolves knew my sorrow as

I lay upon my furs in Ahearn's house, and they called me to them.

I walk close to Kalasin, and soon he begins to run, even-paced and slow, so I can stay with him. He moves unerringly on his invisible course through the forest. He does not stop to sniff or check his direction, but runs as if it is bright day and his way is marked with light. Yet I know that he must read signs; that a hundred smells come to him and are assessed and understood; that he is attuned to all the forest, to everything in it that lives and moves. A badger runs across his path, but Kalasin jumps right over it. We run on, and when my insides ache and my breath comes hard, he slows a little. He is attuned to me, as well.

At last he stops, and I see in the moonlight that we are by a dirt bank in a forest clearing. The ground sloping up towards it is marked heavily with the footprints of the wolves. I see a hole in the bank, and half-forgotten memories sweep over me.

Shula comes out of the den, and sniffs my hands.

"No fish today," I say. She leaps up and places her paws on my shoulders to lick my face. My face is sweating from the long run, and she laps the saltiness on my cheek. Then she drops down again.

Two black bundles come hurtling out of the den, and leap so hard at me that I am bowled over. I roll down the muddy bank, feeling paws and furry bodies and wet mouths on me. I come to a stop and am jumped upon, licked, trampled, and gnawed at. The cubs' teeth are sharp, and I yell. They jump away, and crouch with their noses low, looking sideways at me. I move, and they attack again. This time their teeth catch in my skirt. They wrestle with the folds awhile, and the weave is in shreds when they have finished with it.

Shula barks, and they run back to the den. She follows them in. Though I long to go with them, I stay outside, for it is their home and they have not invited me in. I notice that Kalasin has gone.

I wait a long time outside the den before the songs of the birds herald the sun. The forest springs to life, and radiance dances on leaves and blazes on the earth. Ashok appears, carrying in his jaws the haunch of a deer. Shula comes out of the den, and he drops the meat at her feet. She nudges his nose with hers, whining, as if she thanks him; he mouths her ears and snout, and I feel the great affection between them. Then she carries the meat to a place away from the den, and begins to eat.

The cubs stumble from the den, blinking in the sun. They see that their mother eats, and race towards her; but when they try to drag away the meat, she growls at them savagely, and they run away, whimpering. They go next to Ashok and crouch before him, yapping and whining. His sides bulge with food, and his chest is stained with blood. The cubs sniff at him, even try to poke their snouts into his mouth, begging him for food. He steps back, his head low to the ground, and his sides heave. He vomits up half-digested meat, and Zaal and Zeki tear into it, fighting over the bigger bits.

I am revolted. Then I realise that it is the easiest way for him to bring back meat for three, after a hunt. He cannot drag back an entire deer from whichever far place he caught it, so he brings back a haunch for his mate, and for his cubs he carries the meat in his belly. My repulsion gives way to respect, as I see the wisdom of it.

Ashok, having provided for his family, lies in a pool of sunlight near the den, and sleeps. He has not acknowledged me. I think that perhaps this is a good thing. I could hardly spurn his generosity, should he vomit meat for me.

The sun is high when Kalasin comes back, sides swollen from his feast. He too offers food to the cubs, and they, like human children already full, do not refuse it.

All morning the wolves doze. I begin to think about my life, and about my home. There is contentment for me here with the wolves, but I think I cannot for ever stay with them. I crawl over to where Ashok rests, and I lie full-length in front of him, my chin on his gigantic paws. His face is close to mine. His eyes open a slit, and they are fiery within. I feel again that he pierces my innermost being with his look. I lower my eyes. I know now that it is an insult, or a challenge, for me to look directly into his.

"Ashok, giver of my highest blessing," I say, "I do not know what to do. I love your company, but I think that I have business yet with humans. I am torn inside."

I glance at his eyes again. I keep mine narrowed, give him a sidelong look. His gaze is unblinking, luminous. He closes his eyes, moves his head until his forehead is pressed to mine. His communion heals me, blesses me, and I weep.

After a long time I stand up. The other wolves have gone, either into the cool of their den, or away to the forest to teach the cubs the ways of their world. Ashok stands with me, and watches me sideways. I wipe my face on my hands, and say to him: "If you were a man

I would be ashamed to weep in front of you."

His lips part in wolfish fun. His tail wags, and his eyes dance.

"You may laugh," say I, laughing too, "since you shared my weaker side. I love you well, Ashok, wolf my refuge and my friend. Tell me what to do."

He turns and runs away, slow, so I can follow. I run to catch up with him, and he leads me through the trees. I have no doubt that there is purpose in our journey, that this is somehow his answer.

A long time we run, past startled deer and boar with their great tusks rooting in the earth, and hares with white tails flashing in the sun. We run past a little stream I have never seen before; we skirt marshlands, and I find that I am on familiar paths. We come out of the forest at the place where yesterday Ashok sat and watched me grieving in the rain. We are hidden in the shadows, and no one sees us.

Ashok takes my hand gently in his mouth, and I kneel and press my face against the thick ruff of his neck. He is warm, and smells of the earth. I stand up and look across at the village. The children are playing naked in the moat, their bodies brown with mud. Through the gateway of the fence I see that the women have taken the big wooden bathing-tubs outside. They are filling them with water heated in pots over the cooking-fires. After days of dampness and mud, it is bathing time. Sleeping-furs are spread over the wooden fence to air, and a fire outside burns the mouldy straw from the beds. The young men and girls are out in the fields on the far side of the village, gathering fresh dry grass for sleeping on. I can hear their laughter. I see the youths chase the girls and grab them about their waists, and try to kiss them. A woman in a green dress slips her hand into Gibran's, and he kisses her. It is a long kiss, and the others watch, hooting and applauding. Beyond them the wheat stands straight and golden in the sun.

I turn to look at Ashok, but he is gone.

I find my canoe in the long grass, and paddle back to my human place. My heart is heavy again, like a stone.

11

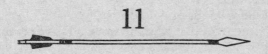

As I pull my canoe onto the bank and walk up between the bathing-tubs, the children fall silent. The women stand up straight and look at me, saying nothing. Their eyes are cold, their lips severe. I think of the light in Ashok's eyes, and wish that I had not come back.

In Ahearn's house it is quiet as death. He is alone here in the dimness, and no one has changed the damp straw beneath his furs. He sleeps, lying on his back, his arms clenched across his chest. His face is oily and wet with sweat; his hair clings to his head. Without a sound I sit by him.

Outside the children shout and play again, and I hear the talk of the women as they pour hot water into the bathing-tubs. I hear the words *wolf-woman*, spoken low, with hate.

Ahearn opens his eyes and looks at me. He has aged twenty summers in these past few days, and his hair is streaked with grey. He says nothing.

"My lord, is there anything that I can do for you?" I ask.

"Give me my sword," he says.

I move back from him a little way, and I can hardly breathe for fear.

His lips pull back on his teeth, and I do not know whether it is a smile or a grimace. "Not for you. For me," he says. "Bury it deep in my heart, Tanith. I cannot live like this."

"I cannot do that, my lord."

"Neither will that whining woman I have got myself. Neither will my useless sons. Nor will Tallil, or that bloody surgeon with his saws and knives. By the gods, Tanith, what will become of me?"

I bend my head, and look at the tattered edges of my skirt, where the wolf cubs have torn it. I have no answer for him.

"Are you not deserting me, like all the rest?" he asks, suddenly furious.

"I will stay, if that is what you wish," I say.

"What I wish! Oh, Tanith! What I wish is that I could roll back nineteen summers, to the harvest-time when I first saw her, all fair and slender in the yellow field. Is our wheat ripe yet?"

"Yes, lord. It will soon be harvest."

I get up, wet a cloth in a pitcher of cool water, and wipe his brow for him.

"Wipe all my face," he says. I wipe his face and hair, and take his hands one at a time and wipe those too. His skin is pale, his nails bloodless like bone. I have never touched his hands before; the feeling is strange to me.

He sighs deeply. "You are more true to me than any of them," he says, very low.

"They blame me for your trouble," I say.

"I know what is true, Tanith. Liam told me the words that went between you and Morag, that night I searched for you. I know she lied. I have told Hrothi and the priest, but they think my mind wanders. Beware, girl. The clan holds you not in its favour."

"It never did, lord."

"It holds you less in its favour now. Look to the man Gibran; if he desires you, marry him. It will release you from our clan, and take you to his. His father has three dark-heads for slaves, and treats them well, I hear. He says they are of more worth to him than twenty cows. You will not be an outsider there."

"I have other friends, lord, to whom I can go."

He opens one eye and looks at me, sideways, as Ashok did. "The wolves, Tanith? You would risk returning to them?"

"I am better acquainted with them than you know, lord."

The skins are flung aside in the doorway, and Hrothi comes in. I move aside, and he goes to Ahearn and pulls back the furs.

"Who neglects this man?" shouts the healer. "Where is his wife?"

I rush outside to look for Morag. I find her with the

other women, scrubbing the backs of the men as they sit in the tubs. She jests with them and blushes at the things they say in return. She looks angry when I disturb her happy work. But when Hrothi sees her he shouts words so full of fury that she hangs her head.

I hide behind the house that shelters our animals at night, for I want to be alone to think. But, though they are hidden from me by the wooden fence about our village, I hear the young people still laughing in the fields beside the wheat, and thoughts of Gibran struggle with my thoughts of wolves.

My new-found serenity is blown away by Ahearn's words about the pledge-son. Only a short time past, all I yearned for was the peace in wolves' company. Now I think of Gibran's mouth and throat and hands, and a madness takes hold of me.

* * *

For three days I do not visit the wolves. I am busy looking after Ahearn, for Morag has deserted him. She gave him back the golden cup, and returned to the house of her parents and family. He spat when she went, and told his sons to smash the bowls and cups she left behind, and to tear her weaving from the loom.

I am teaching Ahearn's youngest son to care for him. Liam is devoted to his father, and learns quickly. I show him how to make medicinal tea for pain, and how to crush roots and seeds for poultices.

Hrothi comes often, and does not approve of my teaching the boy.

"Look after our chieftain yourself," he says to me, early one morning. Ahearn has had a pain-racked night, and I am making medicine for him from freshly gathered wintergreen. I have comfrey flowers in it, too, for the healing of bone. The boy Liam is helping me, his round face frowning and solemn.

"Liam is capable," I say. "He is almost as old as I was when you taught me which plants to give to Nolwynn. He can look after our lord. Besides, I am not always here."

"So I have noticed," he says. "You are already in trouble, wolf-woman. Do not make matters worse by seeking refuge in dangerous and forbidden places."

Liam looks at me, his eyes huge and full of questions. I take the bowl of medicine from his hands. I pass it to Hrothi, and the healer sniffs it and nods his approval. He gives the drug to Ahearn, then says to me: "Will you be here to help with the harvest?"

"Of course," I say. "Everyone always helps with the harvest."

"Everyone, except this man you crippled," he says, and goes.

I am looking forward to the harvest. It is the high time of our summer, when everyone labours in the fields to bring in our ripened wheat. When the work is done, we feast for a night and a day, and offer thanks to the gods that the harvest is safely gathered in and stored. It is the one time when, amid all the celebration and toil, the clan forgets that I am not one of them.

I would look forward to it more eagerly if I thought a friend would work in the field alongside me. Gibran has not even glanced at me these past three days.

12

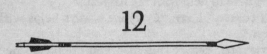

That afternoon, while Ahearn sleeps, I visit the wolves. Zaal and Zeki welcome me with toothy grins and frenzied wagging tails, bowling me over with their unrestrained delight. Then they realise that I have brought a bag of fish for them, and they race off with it, yelping and snapping at one another over the prize.

Shula is more dignified, mouthing my hands and sniffing at the fish smells, then rising with her huge paws on my shoulders to lick my face. Kalasin is reserved: he has a long gash down his side – from a boar's tusk, most likely – and needs rest to heal. I am glad I have brought fish for the cubs, for in fighting over them they keep away from Kalasin.

Ashok simply looks at me. Our empathy is unbroken by our time apart.

I go with the wolves to a clearing not far from our harvest-field. I see the smoke from the village, and the wind carries to me the voices of women and children. The men are absent, and the women are sitting outside grinding the last of the old grain between stones.

The wolves are relaxed. I sit in the sun with them, and watch as Ashok and Shula and the cubs chase harvest-mice in the grasses. They race, twisting and turning in the dust, snapping at the mice as they pounce on them. They catch them, too, and swallow them whole. It is a strange hunt. Afterwards they seem satisfied with their feed, and lie down to rest. I lie with my head on Shula's side, and hear the gurglings of her mouse-meals within her.

"Mighty hunter," I say, and she growls softly, as if she knows I tease her.

Suddenly she grows tense. I see that Ashok is already standing, his head towards the trees nearby. Kalasin too is alert. The cubs, sensing their disquiet, sit up and growl.

I rise to my knees, and see a she-wolf standing in the shadows under the trees. She runs towards us a little way, and is stopped by Ashok. He springs at her, his hackles raised. It is a brief but savage fight, and dust and fur fly. When they part she cringes low before him, her eyes averted, her ears laid back against her head. She snarls, not wholly submissive to him. Neither will she run away. She needs his clan, perhaps, needs protection, and a family. I understand this well.

Ashok bares his teeth, threatening another attack. Still she will not flee. She sinks lower to the dirt, and finally she lies on her side and moves back her head until her throat is exposed. It is the ultimate yielding. Ashok can kill her now, if he wishes.

He does not kill. He straddles her awhile, his teeth just above her offered throat. Then he walks away, stiffly, his tail erect. She is accepted. She rises to her feet and waits quietly while Shula and Kalasin sniff her. Shula is brief, but Kalasin mouths the newcomer's snout, pleasuring her. His tail wags. I think that perhaps he has found a mate.

The new she-wolf stays with us all the day. Kalasin plays with her, and they fight mock battles and tumble together in the yellow dust, until she hurts his wounded side and he snarls at her. Then they lie together to rest, and she licks his wound and grooms him, fondly. The cubs try to join them, but Kalasin bares his teeth at them. They taunt their mother instead, and when she growls they go off to hunt for mice again.

We all play in the sun. The wolves let me wrestle with them, and I roll on the ground with them and sometimes bite them gently; but though their jaws enclose my arms and hands, and sometimes my face, they never hurt me, nor do their teeth leave a single imprint on my skin. Only Ashok does not let me play in the dirt with him.

Evening comes, and the wind brings smells of boar roasting over the village fires. The wolves are restless again, eager to hunt for more than mice, and in my heart I want to go with them. But I am hungry, and the smell of roasting meat is tempting. Ashok comes and licks my face, and I press my brow to his and look straight into his eyes. He knows that I am torn inside, that I ache for things I do not understand. He licks me again, then takes my hand in his mouth. His bite is gentle, but not so soft that I can safely pull away. He holds me there beside him in the forest as the day turns into night, and gives me time to choose.

When he and his wolf-clan run into the darkening world beyond the forest, I am with them.

13

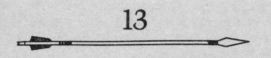

A screen of leaves conceals us from the deer. We are on the edge of a grassy plain, a long way from anywhere I have been before. Beyond the plain are hills, blue in the twilight. The deer are grazing, their young among them, upwind of us, and unaware. It is a large herd. I look at Ashok, wondering when he will begin the chase. Shula has gone on ahead, is hiding somewhere in the long grass past the deer. Ashok knows where she waits. He will chase the deer towards her, and when he tires, she will take over the pursuit and make the kill. Wolves can run fast only in short bursts, and healthy deer outrun them easily; hence this planned attack, this work in unison. I know their plans well, by now:

I have lived with the wolves for ten days. But the thrill of the hunt is always new.

My heart pounds, and my muscles twitch, made too taut by the suspense of hiding. I glance at Ashok. His eyes are half closed, seeing through the deer, through the grasses, searching out the place where Shula hides, sensing her readiness. Soon some unseen signal will pass between them, and in perfect unity they will begin the hunt.

There is a blur in the grass beside me. Ashok is away, running fast and low beside the trees. I sprint after him. The deer lift their heads, are motionless a moment, then flee. Their hoofs thunder on the earth. Out into the open runs Ashok, not too fast, and a little behind the herd. Then, gradually, he moves up beside the deer, spurring them towards the open plain, to the place where Shula waits.

An age, it seems, we pursue them. I pant, breathless, overpowered by this relentless urge to hunt. I am appalled, terrified, elated. I fragment, become the savagery of wolves, the terror of the hunted deer; I am driven, living, dying, powerful, weak. I forget who I am. I become the hunter, craving for the kill.

The herd is spreading out. The little ones stumble and lag behind; the mothers hesitate, their eyes rolled back in fear. Ashok snaps and barks at the flashing hoofs, and the deer leap on across the plain. The wolf is inexorable: he runs them on and on, until at last he tires. Instantly a shadow, arrow-swift, leaps from the grass ahead of him, and the desperate deer, pursued anew by Shula, plunge on. Ashok follows, loping easily, leaving the hunt to his mate. At last a single deer, no longer able to keep up the pace, drops back. Ashok increases speed. Together he and Shula move in for the attack.

Their quarry is a young buck, but not a healthy one. It sweats with terror and fatigue, and its veins stand out along its throat. Its nostrils are distended, hungering. It stops, and Shula, too, hesitates. I know what goes between them, for I have witnessed it in other hunts. It is a moment, a look, of understanding between the hunter and the hunted. The look lasts no longer than a breath, but seems timeless, and encompasses a covenant as ancient and powerful as the hunt itself. In this moment death becomes a choice, a sacrifice. The wolves acknowledge it; and I have seen them abandon prey, after this moment, if the covenant is not made. But this time it is made, and the young deer falters, falls. In an instant Shula has broken its neck.

I sink onto the sun-warmed grass, my lungs on fire and bursting. I am, as usual, far behind the wolves, but I hear Ashok tearing at the deer, and the snapping of bones. The smell of blood is on the wind. I lie on my back and close my eyes. Slowly I relax, and my breath comes more easily. Sweat trickles down between my breasts, and my legs ache. I tremble, thinking of the awful rage to kill that had consumed me. Is that what warriors feel when they go into battle? And are men so much higher than wolves, when swords kill just for pride and greed, but wolves kill for sustenance and life?

The thought of sustenance makes my belly rumble, and I long to return to the den, where I have stored my food. But I must wait until the wolves are satisfied before I approach their kill, then I will help them carry home what is left. I have not eaten raw meat, though I am sorely hungry at times, for the meat is often full of worms, and I cannot bring myself to eat it uncooked. While with Ashok and his clan, I live on eggs and juicy pignuts, and herbs that grow in the forest. I stole some honey once, but the bees were vicious with me. I have learned, with Zaal and Zeki, how to catch fish from the little streams, though the cubs are quicker with their paws, and catch more than I do. They do not share their fish with me, but Kalasin shares his. I slice the flesh from the bones, chop it small, and put it with a salad made from leaves of herbs, and flowers. It is delicious, and I have no ill effects from eating my fish-flesh raw. The herbs help to heal the scratches that I get from playing with the cubs.

I stand up and walk slowly over to the feast. Ashok has finished, and now it is Shula's turn to eat. She has not hunted many times with us, but will come while Kalasin guards the cubs. Kalasin and the new she-wolf are constantly together and there is great affection between them. I have called her Raida, which means enduring one. She is wary of me, and will not yet let me touch her. I think her family was killed by men, and she remembers it. She growls at me sometimes, and Kalasin snaps at her. I make sure I am never alone with her. When we are together, Ashok watches us, his eyes narrowed.

Kalasin and Raida are not often with us now, and I think that one day they will leave to begin a wolf-clan of their own. I will miss Kalasin; he is fun-loving and tolerant, and easy company. He is second in the hierarchy of the wolf-clan, and not so serious and dignified as Ashok. With Kalasin I can wrestle and play, and he enjoys affection. But Ashok ...

Ashok is my great friend, my refuge from the world. Even now, with the fervour of the hunt still in his blood, he is relaxed with me, turning his head towards me and softly mouthing my hand. Not many moments ago these powerful jaws tore apart sinews and bones. I lie near him to wait while Shula eats, and he rests his white muzzle alongside my cheek.

There is great peace in Ashok. In him the spirit of the earth flows free, is understood and honoured. He is attuned with all things. There is a goshawk high in the evening skies; he sees it. A beetle climbs a blade of grass; that he observes. Hunters somewhere in the forest have lit a fire to cook meat; he knows it before he sees their smoke. My heart aches, just a little, for humankind; he knows that, too, and licks my face. He sees it all, knows all things that happen in his domain, and is in harmony with them.

More and more I comprehend this unity that is like a vast web connecting all living things. An intruder places just one foot on the farthest edge of it, and all the web quivers and is aware. Yet everything works together; fights are only to defend territory and are avoided if possible. I have never seen a wolf kill another, nor slay for amusement. A wolf kills only for food. It is the giving and taking of nature, the huge ebb and flow that turns life to death and then to life again.

Even the killing is quick and compassionate. This buck that Shula slaughtered just now has a hind leg half eaten away by an old wound made bad by pus and flies, and it welcomed death. All wolf kills that I have seen are like this. The larger prey are old, or suffering in some way. That is why the wolves hunt together, running the deer until the weak or infirm are left behind, and those they kill and eat.

I shift my gaze to the vast grasslands before us, afire with the setting sun. The deer graze peacefully again, far away from us now, their bodies drenched in light. I wonder what would happen to them if there were no wolves. Would they increase until there was no pasture left for them, so that finally they all would die slowly of starvation? Perhaps the killing keeps all living things in balance. I glance at Ashok. He is tranquil, his eyes full of brightness. So wise he seems, so sure of all his ways. I think how men hunt the wolves for no reason, and how easily they could disturb the rhythm and the scheme of things.

Ashok gets up and goes over to the remains of the deer. Shula has finished eating, and we tear off chunks of flesh to take back to the den, for eating later on. Little is wasted. I carry an armful of meat, and Shula brings a piece of the good haunch. Ashok drags the neck and chest, and, within him, a feast for the cubs. This feed will last the wolves several days.

It is a long walk back to the den, and night falls before we are back in our own territory. Every now and again Ashok howls, and other wolves answer him. I think he says he is on the edges of their territory but means no harm. Sometimes I see wolves' eyes watching us from between far trees, but we are not approached. I wonder if the wolves are so tolerant in winter time when food is scarce, and only the mightiest survive.

A small stream borders our domain, and I stop in it to wash and drink. My clothes are tattered now, and

I have cut my tangled hair short with my knife. Still I wash, because I cannot lose the truth that I am human, and that cleanliness is good. Sometimes Shula washes me when she has finished with the cubs, licking my face and shoulders with her great rough tongue, but I prefer water.

We are almost at the den when we pass through a small clearing, and I see the moon high above the trees, golden and plump like a fruit to be plucked.

"It is our harvest time," I say to Ashok.

I hide the meat in the fork of a tree near the den. The cubs tumble out to welcome us, their paws and noses wet and dripping, for they went fishing while we were gone. Kalasin and Raida too come out, and the wolves all sniff and nuzzle one another, whining, their tails wagging frantically. They all greet Ashok, who stands there like a mighty chieftain accepting rightful salutations from his clan. Then he looks up at the moon and howls, and they all howl with him.

I sing too, my hand on Shula's neck. It is a potent, joyful thing, this howling with the wolves, though there is heartache in it, too, for me, for I know it is a howl for my farewell. In the morning I will go back to Ahearn's clan, to help gather in the harvest. All hands are needed when the wheat is being cut, for if we are slow and it rains while the wheat is on the ground, the grain will be ruined and the clan will go hungry in the winter time.

After our song, Shula and Ashok give the cubs offerings of deer, and while they eat Raida and Kalasin leave the den to go on a hunt of their own. I climb the bank and wriggle into the narrow tunnel to the den. It is not easy to enter this place. The entrance is twice as long as I am, and so narrow that I can only slide in with my arms held out straight in front of me. The tunnel slopes downwards, then widens and goes sharply up to the cave-like den at the end. Here it is warm, and there are hollows in the dirt where the wolves have made their beds. In the pitch blackness I feel for mine, knowing it by the small crab-apples that are there. I munch on them while I curl up and wait for sleep.

I am dozing when the wolves come in, and the cubs battle with me because they think my bed is best and want to share it. We cannot all fit in, so I compromise, and let Zeki curl her back against my front. I sleep with my arms around her, my face between her ears, and feel her breath go softly in and out, and the beating of her heart. I try to ignore the fleas.

* * *

At some time in the night I leave the den to go under the trees to relieve myself. Eyes watch me, and I recognise Kalasin. He is alone.

Standing up, I call to him. He comes, but is hesitant. I bend over him, hugging his neck. His sides are not bulging, and I suspect he has hunted only mice and may still be hungry. "There is meat up in the trees, that I brought back," I say. He pushes his snout against my chin, licks my face. I go to the tree in which I hid the meat, but as I take it down a shadow glides towards me. I see yellow eyes full of fear and jealous rage, and teeth bared for the attack. It is Raida. She growls terribly, and I throw the meat in front of her, thinking that this is what she wants. But she ignores it, her eyes wide and fixed on mine. She means business, this she-wolf.

I wait for Kalasin to rush to my defence, but he does not. At first I am bewildered, then I realise that this fight is between Raida and me, and he will not intervene. Several things I realise, all at once, between two breaths. I know the reason for her rage: I show affection to her mate and offer food to him, and she thinks those privileges are hers. She wants my status in the wolf-clan – the unity I have with Ashok and Shula, and the kinship with Kalasin. She intends not to kill, but to show me she is higher ranked than I am. If I give in to her my relationships with the wolves will alter, perhaps become impossible. I prepare to fight.

She runs at me, snapping, her teeth dripping saliva. I snarl and yell at her, and she backs off. Then she runs at me again. I touch the handle of my knife, but hesitate to draw the blade. In that moment she attacks.

So fast she comes, so powerful and so full of fury, that I can do nothing but raise my arms to shield my face. Her jaws find my right hand, and her teeth in me are agony. Howling, I smite her hard between the eyes with my free fist. The blow stuns her. She backs away, growling and whimpering, watching me sideways. I rush at her and hit her again, hard. I scream at her, hoping rage will blind her to my fear. She looks away, and hangs her head. But she still growls, and I do not trust her. I know I have to tell her now that I am greater, or we will fight again and again until one of us wins. I take her by the ears and shake her head until she yelps. She snaps at my hands, struggling to pull free, and her strength astounds me. I am terrified that she will turn and oppose me in earnest. I let her go, giving her one last hard hit across the neck. She runs, yelping, her tail between her legs.

Kalasin is watching me, his hackles raised. I yell at him as well, and he turns away, his eyes averted. Ashok lies near the den entrance, washing his paws. It is nothing to him: a minor skirmish, a family argument. Yet I tremble all over, and my right hand is pierced and bruised, and bleeds profusely. I collapse on the ground, shaking and sobbing from relief that I am not dead.

When I am calm again the skies are grey above the trees, and the birds are awake. Ashok stands a little way from the den, facing the forest paths that lead back to my human place. He looks at me over his shoulder, his eyes like harvest moons.

14

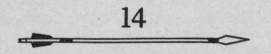

It is a lovely dawn. Ashok stays with me at the forest edge, looking across the moat at Ahearn's village. Everyone is awake and about, preparing for the first day of the harvest. I smell their cooking fires, and know they are eating porridge sweetened with honey, and curds. Someone opens the gate in the fence. I glimpse children wandering outside, drinking cupfuls of milk taken fresh from the goats. The women come out to stand in the sun and talk while they bind up their long hair in rags for coolness. Their voices carry to me on the still morning air. Then the men emerge, making jokes about the slowness of the women, and they all climb into their canoes and paddle across to the open ground. Still laughing and talking, they walk in a procession around to the wheatfields, their sickles flashing in their hands.

Ashok pushes close to me, and I kneel and press my face against his neck. My right hand hurts. Raida's teeth have punctured my palm in two places, and my little finger and the one next to it are crushed and bruised. Ashok licks my hand softly, then backs away from me.

"I am sorry I brought strife to your wolf-clan," I say.

He whines, a high, plaintive sound. I imagine that thoughts pass between us, that I know his feelings as keenly as he knows mine, and then I wonder at my arrogance. I stand up to go to Ahearn's house. Ashok runs back to me, leaps up and licks my face, and is gone.

My canoe is where I left it, half hidden in the grasses. With difficulty I paddle across the moat, holding my hurt hand against my chest.

In Ahearn's house it is dark. The village is silent, for all are gone to the wheatfields save this man. It seems a long time since I have seen him.

I sit by his bed and touch his face. His eyes open, and he stares at me as if he does not know me. He looks at my tattered dress, my bleeding hand, my unwashed face, and he asks: "Did the wolves get your hair?"

Smiling, I answer: "That, and my heart."

He grunts, and shuts his eyes again. His hair is greyer than ever, and he looks old. He reeks of herbal poultices. Near his furs there is a cup half filled with bitter-smelling stuff made from poppy seeds. I offer him a sip, but he shakes his head. "Later," he says. "The day is long."

I pour water from a pitcher into a metal bowl, strip off the remains of my dress, and wash all over. I am covered in scratches, and my knees, shoulders, and elbows are grazed from sliding down the narrow tunnel to the den. I wash my hair, and when I am dry I put on one of Nolwynn's dresses, kept in a wooden box at the head of Ahearn's bed. If Ahearn hears me take it, he does not object. I love this dress; it is saffron-coloured, and the arrows on its hem are woven in blue. From my own belongings I take a red linen girdle which I tie about my waist, and a red leather headband of Ahearn's house. My few possessions are still wrapped in their fox-fur by my bed, and untouched. My lyre too is there. I stroke it lightly with my wounded hand, and think of the howling rituals with the wolves.

Before I put on the headband I tidy my shortened hair with a bone comb that Ahearn gave me when I was a child. I pull on my soft leather shoes, binding the tops around my ankles with cords. It is difficult work with only one good hand. Finally I cut a strip of smooth hide and bind up the wounds Raida gave me.

For a while I stand in this place that has for thirteen summers been my home – stand here with my skin and hair washed clean of wolfish life, wearing the yellow dress of a woman beloved by me, and a headband that marks me as a member of this house – and yet I feel lost. I am between two worlds, and know not where I belong.

Ahearn sleeps. I sorrow for him, for the terrible calamity that has befallen him, for the lie that puts the blame on me and severs me from his clan. Him, too, I loved.

I go outside, get a sickle from the storage house, and paddle my canoe across the moat to the other side.

The fields shine golden in the morning sun. I look at

the bent backs of the harvesters, and I feel more solitary, more alien than ever. The people look up at me briefly, then bend to their work again.

I walk to the far end of the field, near where the wolves and I played a lifetime ago. Though my hand hurts, the reaping work is good for me. It brings me close to the earth again, to the rhythms and reasons of human life. I sing as I cut the wheat, and to my surprise the people around me begin to sing as well, and our sickles move to the tempo of our song.

The sun rises hot and high, and soon sweat runs down our faces and necks. The children bring us bladders of cool water. When we have drunk we tip the rest upon our heads, then set to work again.

After a time I am too tired to sing and work as well. My back aches, and the strip that I have bound about my hand is slippery with blood. I hold the sickle in my left hand, but work clumsily and too slowly. Midday comes, time for us to rest, and I am glad to sit amid the cut wheat, unwrap my hand, and let the sun dry it.

"What – worn out so soon, and hardly started yet?" says a voice that flusters my heart. I flush and hide my hand between my knees. Gibran sits at my right side, so close that I can smell his sweat and feel the heat of him.

"I am not worn out," I say, looking at my feet. One of the bindings is coming undone, and my shoe has almost fallen off. I cannot tie it up again, for then he would see my hand, and I do not want his pity. But he takes my wrist and makes me show him my injured palm.

I dare not look at him. Suddenly I am ashamed of my hair, or what is left of it, and with my good hand I smooth it down against my neck, willing it to grow again. Perhaps he will not notice it.

"I like it short," he says. "It must be easier for hunting and running in the forest thickets. And for reaping wheat."

"It is," I say, and try to pull my hurt hand free.

He holds it more firmly, and says, sounding amused: "So you had a tussle with a wolf. I thought they were your friends, Tanith."

Tanith. My name, Tanith. It is good to hear it again.

"They are my friends," I say. "They are a little rough in play sometimes, that is all."

"Rough? It is a vicious bite!"

"Warriors do worse."

He says nothing to that, but takes a waterskin that he has tied to his belt, removes the stopper, and pours water on my hand. It is cool and soothing on my flesh.

"You cannot work with it like this," he says. "Why have you not asked Hrothi to bind it up for you?"

"I have not seen him. Besides, there is no need. I bound it myself."

He shakes his head. "Let me do it for you this time," he says. He takes the strip of hide from where I dropped it, pours water over it to wash out the worst of the blood and dirt, then spreads it flat upon his thigh. His hands are fine-boned, his fingers slender and strong. He takes my hand and places it palm upwards on his thigh, and gently wraps it in the wet hide. His touch is firm, but does not hurt. My fingers shake; I am like water inside.

I hear the others murmuring about us. One of the young women makes a comment and the youths laugh. If Gibran hears, he does not show it.

"See Hrothi this evening, and ask him to anoint your

hand," he says. "I was bitten once, and Hrothi's ointments healed me in two days."

"You were bitten by a wolf?" I ask.

He grins. "By a ferocious child, when I stole its whortleberries. By your look, you need more than berries. You have grown thin, Tanith, since last I saw you. Have you eaten yet, this day?"

I shake my head, and he takes from a leather pouch beside him a package wrapped in a white linen cloth. He passes it to me. "Wheatcakes made by my own hand," he says. "You have them. I ate well before we left this morning. I do not need them."

Thanking him, I unwrap the parcel. The cakes are good. I try to eat them slowly, making them last. I feel Gibran watching me, and wish we had some words to say.

I finish the cakes and fold the cloth carefully before giving it back to him. He puts it in the pouch, then lies back in the cut wheatstalks beside me, his hands linked behind his head. If he were Ashok I would lie crosswise to him and put my head on his chest, and I would not be afraid nor feel the lack of words. The others of the clan are all lying down, some talking quietly, some dozing. The sun is hot, the shorn earth smells sweet, and the wheat shimmers. I feel in a dream. Beside me Gibran sighs and moves his hand so it rests against my waist. He tugs at my girdle, gently.

"Why not rest, Tanith?" he asks.

"I am not tired," I say. His fingers tug again, and I lie down beside him. Cut wheat stubs prick against my back, and the earth is uneven behind my head. I am too close to him. I can hear his breathing, and feel his hand move in my hair. I roll away from him, onto my front, and bury my face in my arms. I lie very still, though insects crawl on my bare skin and I long to brush them off.

"Tanith?" he says, and I hear the wheat rustle as he moves. I do not answer.

"Tanith? There is something I would talk about with you." He hesitates. "Tanith, you are in trouble with the clan. There is talk. They blame you for this disaster that has happened to our chieftain. I have spoken with the lad Liam, and he says it is no fault of yours, but the people choose not to know that. They want someone to blame." He hesitates again, and his breathing is uneven. He continues, "I know what it is like, living with a clan that is not your own. It is easy for me, since I am the pledge-son, and therefore respected. But you ... your place here is not so easy, I think. I hear what they say of you. But I am not afraid of a woman who has lived with wolves. I honour your courage, and your face pleases me. If you need a helper in this place, think of me. And I would be more than a helper, if you could think of me that way. Tanith? Tanith? Are you asleep?"

I do not move, do not blink, do not breathe.

He sighs and swears, and falls back on the earth again. "Fool, man!" he hisses to himself. "She sleeps! Half this summer I have thought about those words, arranging them! Fool! Fool!"

I cannot help it: my shoulders shake, and I laugh with relief and ecstasy. He grabs me about the waist, and I feel his chin rough between my shoulder and my face, his mouth hot on my neck, his body heavy on me.

"Shame on you, witch!" he cries, his voice muffled against my cheek. "I offer you my love, and you laugh it to scorn."

"I do not laugh at your love," I say.

He turns me over so I face him, and our heads are close. His eyes are brilliant and amused.

"Then what do you laugh at, Tanith?" he says.

"I laughed because you called yourself a fool," I reply.

"And was I a fool, to call myself a fool?"

"A great fool," I say.

"Then the second foolishness cancels out the first, is that so?"

"Sounds wise, to me."

"Then tell me that I am wise, Tanith, before I kiss you."

I am confused, afraid, longing. "It is only wise," I say, "if the others do not watch."

He glances over his shoulder, and turns back again, smiling. "They are all asleep," he says.

Then he kisses me. His mouth is warm, and he tastes like apples. From another world a horn sounds. It is time for work again. He rises, dark against the sun, and offers me his hand. Yonder, watching us, is Sabra, the woman in the green dress.

15

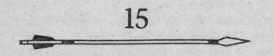

Four days we work in the field. Often I look up at the place where the wolves played, chasing the harvest-mice. I do not see them again, but I see Gibran working further down the field, his back bent, his sickle swinging in his hand. We sit together in the resting time, sharing our meal and laughing together, and he cares not that the others send us sidelong looks and whisper about us. They would not dare, if Ahearn were here. I cannot care. I am all joy.

Even in the nights, when I cook broth for Ahearn and reheat stew for his sons and me, my happiness remains. I hear voices from the other houses, and think of Gibran eating his meat by the fire, his face and arms reddened by the sun, and I am warm inside. I long for the time when our harvest is safely gathered in, for then we will celebrate together, all of us here in Ahearn's house. My lord wishes it, though he is ill. Perhaps Gibran will dance with me. But for now I am content to work with him in the sun, and eat wheatcakes and apples with him.

At the end of the fourth day there is a great shout as the final sheaf is tied. We all go mad, running about and chasing one another, the men catching the women about the waist and kissing them. Always before I have stood apart, for no one chased me. This evening some-one does, and he gathers me close against him and kisses me long and hard, and I am no longer aware of the people around us or the children yelling or the sound of the wind across the stubbled field. It is sunset when we walk home, his arm about my waist.

"Two days more of work there are," he says, "to gather in the wheat and store it. And what will you do then, Tanith?"

My step falters, and his arm tightens about me. "Will you come back to my clan with me?" he asks. "And stand beside me in a wedding feast?"

I cannot speak, can hardly breathe. We stop walking, and he takes my face in his hands. Others walk past us in the dusk, talking and giggling.

"Will you?" he says. I turn my face aside, hiding it against his chest, and try to unravel my thoughts. He waits, smoothing back my hair.

After a long time he says: "You will not be an alien in my clan, Tanith. My father had three dark-heads for slaves, whom he honoured and set free. But they stayed with him, because of his kindness to them. There can be a new beginning for you there, where you are worthy and guiltless. My clan knows nothing of – "

"I am already guiltless!" I say, moving away from him, and walking on. He runs to catch up with me, and takes my arm.

"That I know," he says. "You missed my meaning, woman. Stop, listen to me! I do not understand you. I offer you a fine thing, and you walk away as if it is an insult. What is wrong with you?"

"Nothing," I say, stopping again. I am breathing hard, and my thoughts scramble like the mice when the wolves chase them. "This is too soon, Gibran. I have not thought about this yet."

"How long do you want to think? A day? Two?"

"I do not know."

"What is there to think about? Marriage releases you from your bondage to the house of Ahearn, and it releases me from my obligations as pledge-son. It would suit us both. I like you well, your company pleases me, and your kisses are not too repulsive. Smile, Tanith, I tease you. I love your kisses. I thought that you loved mine. So do you, then, or have you led me on?"

"I have not led you on, Gibran. I would not know how. You began this, remember, with the wolf pelt you gave me."

"Which you burned."

"You know my reason. I ask only for time. My world has changed since the last full moon, and I do not know where my heart is."

"It is because your life has changed that I ask you to be my wife. It is a way out of your trouble."

"I was not talking of my trouble with the clan, when

I said my world had changed. I was talking of my time with the wolves."

"The wolves? By the gods, woman – are you saying *they* have changed your life? Are *they* the reason that you hesitate? Would you rather be with them than with me?"

He is shouting, and I cannot bear it. I walk on quickly, leaving him behind. We are almost at the village, and only one canoe is left on this side of the moat. Getting in, I start paddling to the other side, leaving him stranded. But when he reaches the moat and begins taking off his clothes to swim, I feel guilty. I hold the canoe still in the middle of the moat, watching him. I can tell by the way he flings his clothes on the bank that he is angry. He jumps into the water, and swims towards me. He could walk across, if he wished; the water would hardly come up to his waist. But he swims, then dives under so I cannot see him. I paddle again, all the time looking for him. When he does not appear, I begin to be alarmed. Suddenly a hand slips over the side of my canoe, and before I can blink, I am capsized.

The water is warm from the sun, and churning with mud and bubbles. I feel the canoe bump my head, and then I break upwards into light. He grabs me from behind, pulling me down under the water with him. I struggle, and when he brings me up again he is laughing. He kisses my ear and bites it, not so gentle as the wolves. We stand with our feet in soft mud, water streaming off us like liquid bronze. The children have scrambled up the other side of the wooden fence and are watching us.

"Five days you have, to think," he says. "Is that fair, wolf-woman?"

"It is fair," I say, wondering if it is. He lets me go, and I start looking for the canoe. It is floating half full of water, and I cannot see the paddle.

"Do not worry, Tanith. I will rescue it later. In the meanwhile, let us cool off, and kiss some more."

"Your kisses are hardly likely to cool us off," I say.

He swims over and wraps his arms and legs about me, and pulls me back down under the water with him, where the children cannot see.

The men come out and one of them calls Gibran. He releases me and walks up out of the moat, his back glimmering crimson in the sunset glow. The children giggle and tease him, so he does a crazy dance in front of them, making them scream with laughter. He has gone through the gateway when I come out, dragging the canoe. The children stare at me in silence, and their fathers tell them to go inside. The women too are outside now, watching me. Gibran and I are the last home, but the fires are not yet lit, and there is no smell of cooking in the air. Suddenly I am afraid. I walk up past the people and go into Ahearn's house.

It is dark in here, for the fire is dead. Hrothi and the priest stand silently in the shadows. I look at Ahearn's bed; it is empty, the furs dragged along the floor. Then I see Ahearn. He is collapsed forward on his knees, and the ground is bloody about him, and the blade of his sword comes out through his back.

16

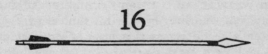

I sit on my sleeping-furs, tormented by hunger and thirst and sufferings far worse. It is late at night; the fire roars, and beside it lies Ahearn, straight and calm and with his sword, cleaned now and shining, laid along his body with its hilt on his chest. He is naked, like a warrior gone fearless into his last battle, his bearskin cloak covering his lower half. Jewelled bands are on his arms, and a golden torque is about his neck. Black fur is under him, and his hair is clean and streams like silk. His hands are folded on his breast, his fingers on the hilt of his sword. Splendid he is, with the firelight playing over him: a king adorned for a last great journey, his eyes open and brave and seeing things beyond us.

They have forbidden me to touch him, so I say farewell to him in my heart while others sing laments and tell stories of him. Gibran sits between two aged warriors, and does not come to me. No one speaks with me, and when they look at me it is with bitterness and reproach.

They sing a triumphal song telling of a place beyond the funeral flames, a land of beauty and peace where people dwell with gods in harmony. In that place there is no death, no suffering, no grief. I look at Ahearn's tranquil eyes, and remember how Nolwynn too gazed so steadfastly beyond. Then the song finishes, and the priest Tallil gets up to speak.

"There is a solemn business to be done," he says, "before we speak our last words of Ahearn, and sing our last farewell, and bear him to his funeral pyre. There has been a shade across this place, a curse upon our clan which we must deal with before our chieftain rises in the wind and spreads his ashes over us. We cannot receive that honour until we have rid ourselves of the evil in our midst."

People begin to mutter, and terror strangles me.

Tallil is handed a leather bag, and from it he takes a small hanging bowl of incense, and amulets made of human hair threaded with the teeth of wolves. He lights the incense and waves it over the clan. The smoke is sweet, sickly, and I cannot breathe in it.

He paces back and forth, reciting sacred words that protect the clan, and all the people whisper their agreement. My heart bangs like a drum; there is a ringing in my ears, and my throat is dry. Then he stops before me, and the house is silent, silent as death. I look at Gibran. His head is bent, and he gazes at his hands.

"I have identified this wickedness, this evil that curses us," says Tallil. He has put down the incense, and only the charms are in his hands, waving over my head. "The evil of the wolves has tangled human spirit with wolf spirit. It has touched our chieftain and caused his death. The curse is here in Tanith."

"That is not true!" I cry. "Ahearn's tragedy was no fault of mine! I went out that night because Morag told me to. She knew where I was, knew that I had gone to fish. There was no need for our lord to go and look for me. There was no need! But she never told him, and he went, and all this grief has come of it."

"You say the fault is Morag's?" says Tallil. "But she loved him!"

"She wanted him when he was well and strong, lord, and not when he was sick. That is not love."

There is a disturbance across the room, and Morag stands. She points at Ahearn's body, her hand shaking. Her voice is high, passionate. "I loved a warrior!" she cries. "I loved this man – this man who lies here now all wrapped in black and gold! I loved him, and when he was injured, weak and weeping like a child, I grieved and could not bear to see him. It was my despair that drove me away from him, not lack of love! And how dare you, wolf-woman, talk of love? Your love is dangerous. You said you loved Ahearn, and look what has become of him! Yours is a love that wounds. It is fatal, and deathly close to the savagery of wolves."

"And it is devious," says another woman, also rising. It is Sabra. Gibran looks up, his face tense. Sabra is not overwrought; she speaks very quietly, and her voice chills me more than Morag's.

"The wolves have cunning," she says. "And cunning is the heart of this one who has run with them. She has killed our chieftain, who took her from the wolves when she was small; now she seeks to destroy his clan. She chooses next the pledge-son. He loved me well, not many full moons ago. Then she came with her wolf-eyes and her guileful ways, and has bewitched his heart. Our two most honoured men has she entangled in her cunning. We are leaderless, lost, and a vital pledge is about to be undone. She plans for us to be wiped out, by men – or wolves."

Gibran moves to come towards me, but one of the old warriors beside him grips his wrist. At last Gibran says: "You are all wrong. There is no blame in Tanith, and no cunning, either. I favour her because she pleases me, because I love her face, and she does not pursue me like other women here. I chose her first, before she looked at me. If she has bewitched me, it is because she did not try to."

"That is part of her cunning," says Sabra. "She has trapped you cleverly, Gibran."

"There has been no trapping," says Gibran. "This evening I asked her to be my wife, and she will not say yes. It is I who would trap her, and she will not be caught."

He looks at me across Ahearn's body, then sits down again. But still I am not easy in my heart.

Sabra remains standing, and slowly she places both her hands on her belly, and stares straight at Gibran.

"You loved me very well, before she bewitched you," she says, smiling a little, triumphant. "I have your child in me, to prove it."

Gibran gazes at her, astonished, bewildered. Slowly

he blushes deep, as if he remembers. He bends his head in his hands and moans.

Some of the men laugh, and one of the old warriors slaps Gibran on the shoulder. "Gather back your heart, man!" he says, chuckling. "The bewitchment is over. A screaming brat will finish it."

My mind whirls. As in an awful dream I see Tallil lifting his arms, waving the amulets high above my head as he chants a prayer against my wickedness. His voice rises, becomes a great shout that booms about the stone walls of the house, and shakes me like thunder. I shrink away, my face turned aside, and his voice vibrates in my heart, through all of me, until I am overwhelmed by it.

"Renounce the wolves!" Tallil commands. "If you refuse, you must go through the rite of exorcism."

I leap up to run, but men fling me against the wall and hold me there. Some of the people scream, and others chant prayers to protect themselves. Across the room Gibran tries to come to me. It takes four men to restrain him.

"Curse the wolves!" Tallil cries. "Curse the hold they have on you! Vow that you will never seek their company again! If you do this, we will forgive you for the tragedy you have caused our clan."

I shake my head.

The chanting swells, rolls over me in waves. Tallil shouts something, but I cannot make out his words. I am taken outside and dragged along the dirt to the fence. They hold me against it so I cannot escape. Soon Tallil comes and stands in front of me. He is wearing a cloak made of a wolf pelt, and the wolf's head, dried and hideous, covers his face like a mask. By wearing wolf skin, he calls into his presence the wolves of the spirit world. He moves charms above me, and prays for protection and power. Then he swings the bowl of holy incense, so that the smoke enters my body to seek out the spirits there. I choke in the pungent fumes, and my eyes stream. About us, the darkness throbs with chanted prayers.

When I breathe calmly again, I see Tallil with a cup in his hands.

"This is the cup of the underworld," he says. "Drink, Tanith, and your spirits will show their true faces. You will give them up gladly."

The men release me. Still chanting, the clan watches. Never have I felt so trapped, so afraid. Tallil has flung back the wolf mask, and his eyes terrify me. He is exultant now, almost ecstatic: this is his true power, his allegiance with the spirits of the underworld. Allied with them, he has total control. Not even the strongest warrior would dare defy him now. I take the cup, and drink. It is bitter stuff, and I cannot identify the herbs in it. I give the cup back to Tallil.

In fear, I wait. I once saw a boy exorcised. He fell on the ground and jerked and choked, and his mouth foamed. He made terrible noises, and they said it was the spirits leaving him. I do not want to do that in front of all the clan. I try to make my body calm, to keep it quiet and under my command.

I wish they would stop chanting. My head begins to ache. My lips feel numb, and I thirst. But when I look for Tallil to ask for water, I cannot see him. It is very dark, and the people seem a long way away. I hear a voice close by my head, whispering about wolves. But the words are awful lies about savagery and hate, and I do not want to hear them.

I am very tired. I need to lie down and cover my head until it does not hurt. But when I try to go back into Ahearn's house, there is a huge void in front of it, that I cannot cross. When I look again, the void and all the houses have vanished.

I am in a forest. Wolves surround me, but they are not the wolves I know. They pace the dirt about me, snarling. More and more appear, until there are so many that I cannot see the ground between them. They close in on me, their fangs dripping. They are evil, full of hate. Their eyes are on my throat, blazing with the lust to kill. When I cover my face, I can still see them. They crouch, ready to attack. Fur brushes my arm. I scream. A wolf leaps –

I am not touched. I cower in the dirt, my arms over my head, screaming and sobbing. At last I have the courage to look up. The clan is watching me, and Tallil swings his holy incense while he murmurs prayers. He seems pleased, as if he approves of whatever it is I have done. He draws near to me, to speak the final words of exorcism. The smoke of incense becomes black crows about his head.

"Evil spirits of the wolf-woman, depart!" he commands. "I send you to the forest depths, drive you into the rocks and stones, and bind you to the wilderness places where you belong!"

He lowers his voice and says to me: "You have seen the true spirits of the wolves. Remember their hatred, their venom, their destructiveness. Be grateful for the kindness of this clan, that has saved you from them, and forgives you. The peace of the gods be with you."

Then he and all the people go into Ahearn's house. I am left utterly alone. Terror fills me. Shadows move all around, and I can still hear the snarling of the wolves. I call for Gibran, but he does not come. No one comes.

Despair and loneliness overwhelm me. I have nothing left: no clan, no human friend, no refuge anywhere. The wolves have torn to shreds my love for them, my trust. Even Ashok would terrify me now.

I cannot bear it. I curl up in the dirt and cry like a child.

I hear a sound, and lift my head. Something small and white comes towards me out of the dimness. As it draws close, I see that it is a lamb. He comes right up to me, bleating. He fills me with love, this lamb, because he is so beautiful, so pure. He glows whiter than the snow, and his eyes are like the sun. Under his gaze my fear is all wiped out, my joy and love restored.

I think of Ashok's eyes, alight with empathy and understanding, and I long for his healing company. In my heart I call to him, whispering his name across the dark. Peace floods over me, and I bow to the ground.

When I lift my head, the lamb is gone.

I rise and go over to Ahearn's house. I do not go inside; I do not think I shall enter these houses again. But the people are beginning to sing, and I stand near the wall beneath the window, to listen. They sing a farewell lament, a funeral song meant for Ahearn. I sing it too, but not for him alone. I sing for Nolwynn, for Ahearn's sons, for all the clan. And I sing above all for Gibran, and desire to see him one more time.

I feel a presence behind me, and in sudden hope I turn around.

The waning moon I see, high above the forest. The ground is smooth and empty to the gateway and the moat, and my canoe waits. And beyond the black water, his eyes shining for me, is Ashok.

17

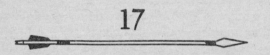

I lie in the dust near the den this early morning, and watch the sun wink down on me through the trees. Nearby Shula sleeps, curled into a ball with her nose hidden in her fur. Zaal and Zeki doze beside her, but they are hungry and getting restless. Their noses twitch, and Zeki chews on something in her dreams. My heart is full of love as I watch them.

I think of those other wolves, sometimes, but now they have no power to frighten me. They belong to a shady, treacherous world that I will not be made to enter again.

The birds are awake, and I enjoy their song more than I enjoyed the sounds of women stirring porridge and complaining at their children. Two moons have waxed and waned since I last heard those human sounds.

With the sunrise, life in the forest changes. The night hunters are home again, and the hares and squirrels appear. New dramas are played out; other creatures celebrate their survival, and search for nuts and leaves and roots.

But not all the hunters are home. Shula gets up, stretches, and goes to stand on the edge of the trampled ground about the den, facing the trees. She stares intently, anxious because Ashok has not yet returned from his hunt. Soon afterwards we hear a long howl that ends in a high pitch. It comes from far away, but I recognise Ashok's voice. Shula's head is raised, her body tense, her ears pricked towards the sound. I too am alert, all my being strained towards his howl.

I am beginning to understand the language of the wolves. At first I understood only what their bodies told. I knew when some small thing in the forest disturbed them, some slight scent in the wind warned them; what was meant by a turning of their ears, a tension, a pause in their step. But now I understand their utterances, and the significance of every yip and growl and bark. Sometimes their wails are so high that I can hardly hear them, yet they carry messages. And then there are the howls. How I have come to love their howls, how I feel myself uplifted and carried high on those resounding harmonies!

One night I went with Ashok to a hill just outside the forest, and he sat there, his body dark against the luminescent moon, and he sang a howling-song. He sang for me, not telling a message or a warning, but howling just because it was his moon, and his heart was full. And I knew, that night alone with him on our solitary hill, why I had always loved the moon and hungered for this freedom in its light.

But mostly the wolves' howls are rich with meanings, and I listen carefully now with Shula, trying to discern what Ashok's howl is telling us. I have the feeling he is saying that he is late finding prey, and will not be back until the sun is high. I glance at Shula; she is suddenly relaxed, her tail wagging from side to side. Whatever Ashok's message is, it pleases her.

It is hard to describe how I know their language. It is something to do with my kinship with the wolves, with that part of myself that has always loved them, that is becoming more and more attuned to their memories and their ancient knowledge. Perhaps I did know their language once, but had for a while forgotten it, and now I remember. This remembering is mystical and deep and powerful; it is something I know in my heart and not in my head.

But the wolves' truest communion lies in their vast awareness of themselves and each other, in their profound intuitive sense of where their kinsfolk are and what they do. It is this empathy that is their great strength.

Shula's eyes glow. Something passes to me from her: an assurance, a promise that all is well.

"I know it is," I answer her. "I understood his message, I think."

Her look is one of utter peace; she knows she has heard him aright. The cubs growl softly in their dreams, and their empty bellies rumble. I realise that I too am hungry. When Ashok is back, Shula and I will leave the cubs with him and go to the stream. I miss Kalasin and Raida, who might have minded the cubs for us. They have been gone two nights now. We heard them howling yesterday, and I knew they were outside our territory and near a harvest-field, where mice were plentiful.

Dozing in the sunlight, I think of human things. A presence penetrates my dreams, and I glance up and see Ashok. The sun is halfway to its zenith.

Shula is on her feet, springing to welcome him. Whining with pleasure, she licks his face, presses her nose against his chin and into his neck, and places her forefeet on his shoulders, embracing him. He pretends to be aloof and merely tolerant of her wild affection, but then his tail wags, and he nuzzles her. Always she welcomes him like this. Sometimes he forgets he is the chief, and plays with her as if they are two cubs, rolling down banks and into long grasses, grunting and whining in their bliss. I have never seen him mate with her, for this is not their season for it, but their kinship is strong and beautiful.

I wait with the cubs, and when Shula has finished greeting him Ashok comes to them and lets them leap up at him and nip him. They are merciless in their affection, attacking any part of him where they can sink their jaws. He is so patient with them, so tolerant. They are still fluffy and fat, but a good deal bigger than they were when I first saw them.

While Ashok's cubs greet him, Kalasin and Raida arrive. I smell on them the dust of wheatfields, and yellow straw and grain are entangled in their fur. They nuzzle Ashok, their heads bent low beneath his, then Raida goes into the den to sleep. I am glad, for it means that Kalasin and I can have a time without her eyes on us. He leaps up on me, his paws heavy against my shoulders, and knocks me to the ground. His tongue is all over my cheek, and then he takes my head in his jaws and forces it against the earth. I lie still, my life in his power. It is Kalasin's way of saying that he is older kinsman to me, and I must remember it. Ashok too does this to me sometimes, when I greet him, as he does to other wolves, to say that he is wolf their father, wolf their chief. In yielding, the subdued wolf accepts Ashok's authority. It is a vital rite.

The lives of all wolves are filled with rituals – the ritual of the howling-song before a hunt; the ritual of taking turns to eat, with the chief wolf eating first; the guarding and grooming of cubs; the marking of territories; this exuberant greeting time; and many others yet unlearned by me. All are signs of their unity, their allegiance and obedience to their chief. The rituals signify their communion, their soul.

After a while Kalasin releases me, and we roll together in the dust, my arms about his neck. Then he too goes into the den, and I see that Ashok has regurgitated part of his meal for the cubs. While they feed, Ashok comes to greet me. He presses his nose against my face, sniffs my hair and neck, and allows me to bend my head beneath his snout and embrace him. I wish that he would greet me as Kalasin does, tumbling in the dirt with me, but understand that this is beneath his dignity; or perhaps he keeps his most devoted caresses for Shula. Whatever his reasons, his gentle salutation is enough. Then he lies down in the sun with Shula, and they are fond together. She and I will feed soon, down at the stream on the edge of our territory, where the fish are fat and slow in the warm shallows and the watercress is sweet.

I stand in this shining place, the wolves at ease about me, and feel so blessed that I raise my arms to the sky and sing a song of praise. Zaal and Zeki howl to accompany me, their soot-black noses raised and glistening in the sun, their little faces frowning with the effort of their wails. Ashok opens one solemn eye and looks at them, and I think he does not approve of our untuneful caterwauling. I laugh and fall upon the cubs and hug them close to me. In an instant they are on their feet, raring for a game, and I race ahead of them to play tag about the trees. At last, exhausted, they return to the den to sleep, and Shula and I go to the stream.

For once Ashok comes with us, leaving Kalasin and Raida to guard the cubs. He walks around the limits of his territory, and we go with him for company. He checks his signs that he has placed on the bushes and trees and clumps of grass that border his land, and he renews them, spraying a little urine again on each place as a signal to other wolves. This is my hunting ground and these are my paths, he says.

Shula and I walk within his territory, on narrow ways worn down by huge wolf feet. I place my foot within the print of Shula's paw; only my toes extend beyond it. I am frail compared with her. She knows my thoughts, and turns and barks at me.

"I am not too frail for a race, though," I say, and clap my hands. She begins to run, swift and silent. The pace is slow for her, but I run hard to keep close behind. Out of the corner of my eye I see Ashok running with us, stopping often to mark his boundary. There is power running with the wolves, and awesome unity.

We come to the stream and I pull off my yellow dress and bound into the water. Because it is shallow I lie down in it, letting it gurgle and ripple over me. I sing as I lie there, a silly, high song about a trout. At the edge of the stream Shula and Ashok watch and listen, their mouths open and their pink tongues hanging out.

"No need to laugh," I say. "I sang for a chieftain's wife, and for a clan on feasting-nights. My voice is not so rough."

Ashok half closes his eyes, and comes down to the water to drink. Shula too drinks, standing chest-deep in the stream, her nose near my feet. I tickle her face with my toe, and she bites me softly. We fish for a while, and the wolves have a good feed. I am able to seize only one fish, but it will make a good meal later.

When we have fished we lie on mossy rocks to rest. The forest is still and cool about us. A patch of sun lies on my left breast just by my heart, and I look down and think how brown I have become. I often lie naked in the sun now, to dry after I have bathed, or just to rest on the edges of the forest. I need my dress when I run along Ashok's paths, for he runs lower than I do, and his paths are crossed by thorns and branches that slash at my shoulders and arms. I do not go beyond his territory if I can help it. If I am alone and do stray from his domain, he howls to warn me, and to tell other wolves that I am not a hunter and am only passing through.

The wolves' understanding of me leaves me amazed and humbled. I have only to think a thing, to feel a fear or a hurt, and they know it. Yet I miss human company, and am angry with myself for missing it. There is conflict in me. Ashok knows, and lifts his head to place his muzzle on my chest. I stroke his soft ears, his massive brow.

"What do I miss, wolf my kinsman?" I ask. "Do I miss the fury and the fighting, the stories of war and the songs of strife? Do I miss the clan's distrust, its scorn of me, its blame? There is not one there who loves me now. Only one, perhaps, but he loves another more. Oh, Ashok. Why can I not comprehend humankind? They misjudge me, taunt me, deceive me, kill me slowly with their love and quickly with their hate. Tell me that I am mad to long for them."

His tawny eyes blaze into mine. Then, in a single fluid movement, he stands and leaps off the rock into the sandy shallows of the stream. Bright droplets spray about him; he crouches low on his forelegs, and his tail, swinging back and forth, makes the water fly. Grinning, whining, he watches me sideways. He lifts one dripping forepaw, whines again. I understand. I am astounded: Ashok wants a game!

I fling myself into the water, and all my longing for human company is forgotten as, for the first time, I roll and wrestle with him like a cub.

18

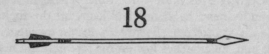

The wolves are asleep in the sun outside the den. Only Ashok is not here: he has gone off on some business of his own. It is hot today, and I long for the cool waters of the stream. I know where berries are, too, that I can eat.

Shula opens her eyes and stares at me, knowing my intent. Her tail wags in the sunny dust as I get up and sneak away, hoping the cubs will not wake and try to follow me. Too late: I am not a stone's throw from the den when they come hurtling along behind me. They leap up at me, whining, imploring me to take them too. They know I have the stream in mind, and they are thirsty. They are too young and inexperienced to go there alone, and I cannot deny them. I look back at

Shula; she is unconcerned, trusting me with them. So we leave, the cubs racing pell-mell down the familiar path, pouncing on every leaf that moves, every beetle and dragonfly.

The forest is breathless, shimmering. Zaal and Zeki hide in the undergrowth beside our path, and as I pass they pounce on me, then bound off ahead to hide again. They are experts in ambush, and I am never wholly prepared for them. Their energy exhausts me.

On the way to the stream I leave the path and pick some berries. They are warm and sweet, and the juices run down my chin and onto my naked body. I have left my dress in the den today. The cubs are engrossed in watching a bee busy about some yellow elfwort flowers, and I can tell they are planning an attack. They learn all things the hard way, Zaal and Zeki, but what they learn they remember. While they do battle with the bee, I creep away and half hide between the trees. I call the cubs, and see them lope towards me, black balls of fur bouncing through the trees. They halt, looking in my direction, their noses twitching. They have got my scent, but cannot distinguish me from the trees all about. I hold my breath, waiting for them to find me.

It is a game we play. I have discovered that the wolves do not find me easily when I stand perfectly still among trees, yet if I move they see me in an instant. I call to the cubs, then see how long I can stand without giving myself away. It is a long time today. They walk towards me, their ears pricked, their mouths slightly open. I love the sight of them, and I grin. That is all they need; they come bounding towards me, and I brace myself against the force of their greeting. Still I fall over, and they lick my face and throat as if they have not seen me since the last full moon.

The stream is cool and refreshing. The cubs and I are chasing one another in the shallows when a sound stops us: a wolf howling in the distance. Immediately Zaal and Zeki are on the sandy shore, quivering with fear. They do not even shake themselves dry; more vital things are in the air. The howl comes again, and they dash down the path back to their den, gone before I am even out of the water.

I race after them, my heart pounding as if I am a deer pursued. It was not Ashok's howl: it was the black wolf in the territory west of ours, and he calls to warn us of hunters leaving his area and entering our own. The hunters are human, and there are many. They are on our south-west border, heading in the direction the sun sets, and their intent is evil. All this is told in our neighbour's howl.

As I run I hear Ashok call, warning me to bring the cubs back home. I howl, and hope he understands that they are already halfway there. But my howl is an impotent thing, for my lungs are on fire with the hot dry air, and I have no breath. By the time I reach the den I am drenched in sweat. I can hear the cubs yelping inside, but Shula is outside with Kalasin and Raida, and they all are standing stiff and aggressive, their ears laid back. Suddenly Shula howls. I hear Ashok answer her. He is a long way away. His howl has warning in it, telling her to stay and guard their home while he confronts this danger that stalks his territory.

Fear overwhelms me. I shake, and my legs feel like water. Raida is shaking too, and soon she whines and runs into the den. Kalasin follows her. Ashok's howl commanded him to stay as well, though he longs to go to his leader's aid. Shula stays outside the den with me, quivering with apprehension for her mate. Suddenly she turns and bolts inside.

I cannot go in; I feel attuned to this terrible thing in Ashok's territory and, though it strikes cold fear in me, I cannot hide from it. And then I know why: it is because it is a human thing. I slide into the den and get my tattered yellow dress. Warriors go naked into battle sometimes, to prove that they are fearless, but fearless I am not. I slither out of the den and pull on the dress. Then I run to find Ashok.

I do not have to think where he is. With every part of me I am aware of him, of his presence. He is a long way from the den, in a part of the forest where we do not often go, for it borders the hunting ground of other wolves. I find him standing in a thicket, his body tense and aggressive, all his hackles raised. He does not growl, but he pants in expectation, teeth bared. I crouch beside him. The forest is hushed, waiting.

And then comes the tumult. It is worse than my darkest dreams. I hear women shriek, and the sounds are horribly cut short. Men shout in rage and pain, and swords clash. Children wail, and animals scream. The clamour echoes through the forest, shaking the trees and the earth and stirring up the air with the stench of strife.

At last the screaming is over, and I hear only men shouting and cheering. It is the laughter of the victors. The air is filled with the smell of fire and the odour of burned flesh. Soon all is silent again. Smoke rolls towards us through the trees, and I am afraid the forest is on fire. But if it is, Ashok does not understand, because he starts to go forward into the smoke, into the place of death. He must see for himself this ugly thing that has happened in his domain.

I stand to go with him, my hand on his neck. He goes cautiously, his nose close to the ground beneath the acrid smoke.

We come to a ploughed field. It has been trampled by horses, and crows peck at the seeds that lie exposed. Beyond the field are houses on fire. The fence around them has been smashed, and through the broken spaces I see smoke billowing across the ground. I see men crucified against trees, arrows through their hands and feet, and women transfixed with spears to the earth, their lower bodies bare and bleeding. There are children covered in blood, or lying in fires, and hens and goats slaughtered.

I turn and stumble back into the forest. The smoke stifles me, and my head spins. I lean on a tree and vomit. Ashok presses against me, and I fall beside him and weep into his fur. He is calm now that he knows what has happened in the forest. He has probably seen it all before. But I have not. I have only heard warriors telling stories and chuckling over their ale while they celebrated their victories. And I am ashamed, ashamed that I once thought their tales were wonderful.

* * *

I am sad tonight. Ashok, Kalasin and Raida have gone out into the darkness to hunt, but Shula stays with me. She knows I have seen enough of death. She licks my cheek, and I lie on my back with my head close to hers, and feel her breath go in and out across my face. After a while she lowers her head and rests her nose on my hair.

Clouds drift across the moon, and somewhere a wolf howls. Shula whines and bumps her tail against the earth. It is Ashok, telling us that he has hunted well.

I think of vegetables baked in embers, and wheat-cakes made by my beloved's hand. I sigh, remembering that he is not my beloved. He belongs with another who wears all green and has a greater claim on him than I do. I think of Ashok. He has two she-wolves in his clan, yet he is loving only with Shula. They have a greater loyalty, wolves.

"He is a fine man, though," I say, and I ache for him.

* * *

Two days later we take the cubs for a walk in the forest, along the southern border of Ashok's territory. It is a learning time for the cubs, though I too discover the world anew, becoming more and more aware of smells and changes in the wind. I find late summer's fruits and berries, and eat well.

On this day Kalasin and Raida leave us.

We are near the edge of Ashok's domain, and the wolves begin to sniff noses and to yip and whimper at one another. They are very affectionate, all of them. Lastly Kalasin comes to me and leaps up with his paws on my shoulders. He licks my face and neck and chest, and I know it is his farewell. I hug him and we roll a while in the leaves and undergrowth, both of us whining. Even Raida farewells me, for she is easy with me now. We watch them vanish into the next territory.

Shula's head hangs low as we walk back, and Ashok walks so close to her that his shoulder nudges hers. The cubs bound on ahead, not fully realising that they have lost their most faithful and tolerant playmate.

We are still a long way from our den when the black wolf in the western regions howls to tell us that there is an intruder in our territory. A lone man. Ashok howls back to say that he has heard, and all seems well. But I am troubled by a sense of foreboding. Ashok leaves Shula's side to walk next to me. I put my hand on the thick ruff of his neck, and his peace flows into me. But as we near our den he hesitates, and I feel the hairs rise along his spine. Immediately the cubs turn and come back to him. He has made no sound, yet they know his caution.

In utter silence we go on. At the edge of the trees we stop and look towards the entrance to the den.

A man sits there, crosslegged, his spear across his knees. He has not seen us yet; his hands are folded in front of him, and his head is dropped low on his chest. He has been waiting long, and dozes in the heat.

It is Gibran.

19

No sound do the wolves make. They stand with me, still and silent as the trees, and all I can hear is my own breathing, quick and distressed. At last I speak his name.

In an instant he is on his feet. He looks at me, astonished and alarmed, and his eyes move down all of me. I remember that I am naked, and even though he has seen me and all the women in our shared bathing times, this is somehow different. I feel vulnerable and shamed. "Close your eyes," I say.

"Not with them there," he says, pointing with his spear at the wolves.

"They will not hurt you," I say, and run up the slope to the den. I slither inside, and he says something that

I do not hear. I feel in the darkness for my dress. I tremble, and my mind is in disarray. At last I touch the woven material, but my hands are shaking so much that it takes an age for me to put it on. I run my hands through my unkempt hair, and search the floor again for the red headband of the house of Ahearn. I cannot find it. I lick my palms to smooth down my hair and wash my face, but suspect I only smudge on more dirt. I am angry and confused, and decide that I will not go out again.

There is a shout outside, a cry of terror. The sound is muffled in the tunnel, but I understand its meaning. I wriggle out of the den to find Ashok standing close to Gibran, staring up into his eyes.

Ashok is not growling, but neither is he wholly relaxed. Gibran's face is white, and his hands on his spear are quaking. I am glad he is afraid; it gives me back my power.

"Why have you come?" I ask.

"Send the wolf away," he says, so tense that his lips hardly move.

"Why? He is only welcoming you. It is warmer than the welcome he first gave me. But I would crouch in front of him, if I were you, and not look so fixedly at his eyes."

"I will not bend the knee to a wolf. Call him off. He is going to attack."

His fear is so acute, so needless, that I cannot help smiling. "So? You have your spear. You will have to be quick; he goes for the throat."

"By the gods, Tanith! If I kill him, they will all be on me! Call him off!"

I do not need to. Ashok has already decided that the warrior is harmless. He turns away, almost scornfully, and lies down under the trees with Shula and the cubs. All the wolves are tranquil, taking their lead from Ashok, and perhaps from me. Gibran will not move his gaze from them.

I sit on the dirt in the sun, and brush the soil from my hands and arms. I had not noticed before how stained I got, crawling in and out of the den. I remember that I have not washed since yesterday's yesterday.

At last Gibran sits by me, not comfortably, but squatting with his spear in his hands, ready at any moment to leap up and defend himself.

"Why have you come?" I ask again.

He dares to move his gaze from the wolves, and looks at me. I had forgotten how blue and clear his eyes are, how beautiful his face. There is a long cut down his cheek, only a day or so old.

"I need to know your decision," he says.

"What decision?"

"Have you forgot? By the gods, woman! Whether to marry me, or not."

I stare at him, astonished, unable to speak.

"I have been waiting for your answer!" he cries, suddenly angry. "Five days I gave you. Two full moons have come and gone, and I have been waiting."

"I thought all that was nothing now," I say, "since Sabra has got your child in her."

"She lied. The cycle of women is with her again. She has no child. You have mistaken everything, Tanith. It is you I love."

"Then why did you believe her when she said she

had your child? I saw your face. All the clan saw it, and knew your guilt. I knew then that your heart was not with me."

"My heart *is* with you, Tanith! With you, and not with her! It's that other part she got. Well, I think she did. I am not sure. Anyway, it matters not. I have rejected her, in front of all the clan."

"You are not sure? How can you do that with her, and not be sure? Did you lose your mind to her, as well?"

"No! I was confused by ale! It was the night of our victory-feast, the night before Nolwynn died. I drank too much. I remember that I went outside, and two women followed me. I think she was one of them. I remember – I think I remember – it is a muddle in my head ... that they – we – in the wheat in the storage house. I don't – "

"*Both* of them? In the wheat? Gibran!"

"I don't know! It might have been neither of them. I was probably incapable."

We are silent, and he stares at the wolves again, warily. The cubs are asleep, but Ashok and Shula are watching us. Ashok is standing, his hackles raised because we are shouting, and he knows there is anger between us. My head and heart are bound with Gibran's feelings, and I am only half mindful of the wolf.

"I wish you had not come here," I say. "I thought that you had chosen her, and that was the end of it. I was happy with the wolves, with my life here. I wish you had not come."

I weep, and am furious with myself for it. My two worlds clash in him, causing me pain. I force myself to speak on. "I will not be your wife. I do not wish to return to the clan."

"There is no reason for you to return to your old clan. You would come to my clan, with me. You will be accepted there."

I look at him. His face is earnest, his cheek swollen with the new wound. "Why has Hrothi not healed your face?" I ask.

"He is dying. He took an arrow in the chest. Six of us were hurt. We fought badly without Ahearn's leadership. His firstborn, the pledge-son, should be brought back to lead the clan. But he is a herdsman now, gentle like his mother Nolwynn, and cannot fight. When the old men are not grumbling about their injuries, they talk about who should be chieftain next. We have problems, Tanith."

"Can you not heal yourselves?"

"We try. But only Hrothi knows the purposes of the herbs. Young Liam mixes us potions for pain, but he cannot stop badness in wounds, or fever."

"Why were you fighting, if you were so unorganised? Were you attacked?"

He laughs. "No one would dare attack *us*, even when we are unorganised! No. We raided a village, only two days past. Why?"

I jump up, and begin pacing the dirt outside the den. "I saw what remained, after your raid! Oh, Gibran, I cannot understand you! Men are so treacherous, so terrible!"

He sits there staring at me. He does not understand.

"I cannot go back with you!" I cry. "I cannot abide the way you live, the thing you call bravery, and the fickle way you love. I cannot understand your words, your actions, your heart."

He throws down his spear and stands to confront me. "What have I done wrong, now?" he cries. "I tell you that we have raided a village, and you turn on me like a rabid she-wolf! By the gods, Tanith, you perplex me! I walk a day through the forest, tracking you – I risk my life facing wolves, to talk with you – I offer you my love, my life – and you tell me I am fickle! Well, I am not! I have suffered the clan's mockery for you, taken their taunts and their ridicule! To marry you I am giving up my place as pledge-son – giving up the home I have had these past thirteen summers, and returning to my own clan, to be just another son, to plough fields and scatter grain. For you I do this – for you, so I can call you wife, and sleep with you in my arms at night, and have my children by you! That is not fickle, Tanith!"

"I did not say you were fickle! I meant that all men are, that I cannot understand human beings any more! I have changed, Gibran!"

"You may have, but I have not! I love you, Tanith! It hurts, when you mock bravery and strength, and say I have no heart! I have not come here to be mocked and spurned!" He takes my shoulders in his hands, and shakes me. "I came to see a wife, a face I love – "

A dark force knocks him aside. It is so fast, so violent, that before I realise what has happened, he is on the ground, Ashok's teeth in his shoulder. Gibran's hand goes for his knife. Dust flies, and the air is filled with the growls of the wolf, and the desperate shouts of the man. Then I see Gibran lying over Ashok, his left arm across the wolf's throat, his knife lifted high. I grip his wrist with all my strength, and twist until he yells and drops the knife. It skids across the dirt, and Gibran swears and flings himself after it. Before he reaches it Ashok is on him again, claws tearing down his back. Blood springs up in scarlet stripes. Gibran rolls over, and his hands find the wolf's throat. He is panting with effort and pain.

Ashok wrenches free. There is a fury of dust and fur and blood, and then Gibran is lying on the ground, Ashok's forepaws on his chest. The wolf growls, his head hanging low over the man, for they are both exhausted. Gibran sobs with agony and fear. He lifts his lacerated arms to defend himself, but they fall back on the dust. Blood runs down his face as he looks at me.

"Get my knife, Tanith," he whispers. "Kill him. Please."

"I cannot," I say, my face wet with tears. "I cannot."

As I speak, Ashok moves away, his tail high and proud. Dumbfounded, Gibran lifts his head and watches him go; then he collapses on the dirt again, his eyes closed. I kneel by him, appalled by his terrible wounds. He is scratched and torn all over, and Ashok's teeth have pierced the soft skin above one eye. The eye itself is whole, but blood fills the socket and flows down Gibran's cheek. Dirt and blood are all over him, and he shakes so much that his teeth rattle.

I cannot touch him. I see the knife in the dirt, and feel the guilt of betrayal. "I am sorry," I say.

"Not so sorry as I," he says. "I knew you loved the wolves, Tanith, but I did not think you would aid one to kill me."

"He would not have killed you," I say. "He was only defending a member of his clan. When you took hold of me he thought you were attacking me. He wanted only to stop you."

"You have more faith in him than I have. If I had kept my knife, that savage brute would be dead now."

"That is the difference between wolves and men," I say. "Those savage brutes show mercy."

He sighs deeply, and looks at me through his undamaged eye. To my amazement, he grins. "Since you would not be my defender," he says, struggling to sit up, and groaning with hurt, "you can be my physician, and bandage me up."

I help him to his feet. He leans on me heavily, his arm about my neck trembling with fatigue, his breathing shallow. My dress is stained with his blood.

"There is a stream not far from here," I say. "You can wash there, and I will bind leaves on your scratches to stop the bleeding. Then I will walk home with you."

"Home, Tanith?" he says, as we walk slowly past the wolves. "Which home?"

"To yours, with Ahearn's clan," I say. "I will not go with you to your clan, and I will not marry you."

As I say this, we pass Ashok. He lies close to Shula, his fur grimy with dust and smeared with Gibran's blood. But his eyes, when he looks at me, are full of secret wisdom. I wonder if he understands my words to Gibran, and is amused by them.

* * *

Gibran steps into the stream's shallow flow, stoops, cups his hands, and drinks deeply. As he stands up, he gasps with agony. Each time he moves the scratches down his back bleed afresh. He removes his boots, belt, and torn and bloodied tunic, throwing them all on the rocks near the stream.

"Dressed like a brave warrior for battle," he says. "Only the battle is over, and I am more wounded than I have ever been. In truth, Tanith, I had rather fight an entire village on my own than that wolf of yours."

"I admit, his claws and teeth are more lethal than the looms of women and the cries of helpless children," I say.

He gazes at me steadily, his face inscrutable. Then he begins washing himself, and the water sounds peaceful as it pours from his hands and trickles over him. The air is taut with our disunity.

"Do you despise us so much?" he says.

"I pity you," I say.

I sit on a rock to crush the healing plants that I have gathered on our way. I press the leaves gently, and out of the corner of my eye see Gibran sitting in the stream, groaning as the flowing waters cleanse his wounds.

I tear wide strips from the hem of my dress and wash them, then enfold the bruised leaves in them. I do not have enough for all his cuts, but the bad ones on his back and chest I can bind. He comes out of the water, washes his tunic, and drapes it on a sunny rock to dry. Then he crouches next to me and watches my preparations.

"What are your medicines, healer woman?" he asks.

"There are blackberry leaves to stop bleeding, purple burnet flowers for healing, and mousewort leaves to prevent foulness in the wounds," I say. "Though I cannot promise that they will be effective. Stand up, and hold your arms out straight in front, so I can bandage you."

It is a strange feeling, binding him, being so close to his nakedness. I have been so long with wolves that I had forgotten what it is like to touch another human's skin. And I had forgotten what he is like.

"I have dreamed of this closeness, Tanith," he says, as if he reads my thoughts, "but I had not reckoned on the blood and hurt. My plans are sorely cut back."

"So are mine," I say, and I cannot help returning his smile, for it has warmth in it, and wickedness.

"What were your plans, Tanith?"

"To go hunting tomorrow with the wolves."

"Hunting what? Boar? Deer? Or the mighty bear?"

"The mighty harvest mice," I say, "while they are still about."

"Mice! Ha, Tanith! Is that what your fierce wolves thrive on? Mice?"

"You may laugh, warrior. The wolves do us a service, keeping down the numbers of those that steal our grain."

He is silent, thinking, and I take a thinner bandage and tie it about his head, over his wounded eye. He slips his arms about me, and when I am finished he kisses my hair, my forehead, my cheek. I turn away before he has my mouth, and hand him his tunic. He puts it on, then his leather belt with its empty sheath.

"I would go back for my knife and my spear," he says, "but I think it is not worth the risk."

"I have a knife," I say.

He gives me a strange look. "You have changed your tune, singer," he says. "A short while back you would have allowed my death, and now you will defend me? I do not understand."

"I have already told you, Ashok would not have killed you. You were in no danger. I carry my knife against poisonous things, and to slice meat."

He smiles. Before he can say something mocking, I kneel before him and bind on his boots. He is still smiling when I stand. His amusement angers me.

"What you call danger and what I call danger are two different things," he says.

"True," I say, beginning to walk in the direction of the village. "You and I are different, Gibran. There can be no meeting of our ways. I have chosen the wolves, and that is an end to it."

He limps to catch up with me and takes my hand, forcing me to walk slow, beside him. I feel a great weariness in him.

"I say it is not the end of it," he says. "I have not had a fair chance, Tanith. A long time you have lived with the wolves, knowing them, being at ease in their company. You and I have spent but a few days in harmony, and you know me not. At least give me an equal opportunity to prove my worth. Then choose between the wolves and me."

"I have lived in a human clan for nearly all my life," I say, "and I had rather be with wolves."

"You have lived with Ahearn's clan. His people are hard, unforgiving. My clan is easier. I swear it, on my father's honour. We are not a warlike family – that is why we wanted a pact with Ahearn, so that we could live peaceably alongside him, and in the hope that he would defend us if others attacked our clan. My father's people have different gods from Ahearn's clan. Their priest teaches only about the god called the Lion and the Lamb. Give me a chance, Tanith. That is all I ask."

"You ask for too much," I say, and he sighs heavily and puts his arm about my shoulders. We have not walked far when I become aware of Ashok's presence. In utter silence he follows us, making sure that the man does not attack me again. I do not see him, for he follows at a distance, and is wary; but I know he is there and anxious for me, and I send him my peace.

It is growing dark, and we are still a way from the village. Gibran breathes heavily, groaning with every step. "Lie down and rest awhile," I say. He falls onto the grass, trembling uncontrollably. His lips are dry and cracked. We are far from any streams, and I fear for him, for he has lost much blood. I wish I had a cloak to cover him, or flints for a fire, because autumn breathes its first chill upon our nights. I cannot hold him to warm him or I will press against his hurts. I sit beside him, close, and watch the crescent moon rise beyond the trees. Ashok comes to sit in front of me, his eyes and his white muzzle luminous in the gloom.

Gibran sleeps, shivering, lying awkwardly on his side with his arms about his head. After a while Ashok lies down near his back, warming him with his soft fur. The moon is high when Gibran wakes and sees me watching him. He reaches out his hand to me. I enfold it in both mine; his flesh is cold.

"I think I can walk on again," he says, his voice hoarse because he thirsts. "Though it is comfortable here. What is it that lies soft and warm against my back?"

"The wolf you fought," I say.

Gibran whispers: "Will he snap my neck if I move?"

"I think not," I say. "He is a gentle bed partner."

I help Gibran up, and he stands staring down at the wolf. Ashok is awake, relaxed, his eyes blazing. Gibran half smiles, and says: "I thank you for your warmth, grey wolf. I had rather your fur than your claws against me."

Ashok wags his tail and bares his fangs in an awful grin. Gibran backs away, stumbling, and I support him with my arm. "Lean on me again," I say. "We are but a short walk from the village. I can smell their fires from here."

Gibran sniffs the air, then shakes his head. "You have a wolf's nose, Tanith," he says. "And a wolf's eyes, which I love." He tries to kiss me, but I turn away. We keep walking, and Ashok is beside us, next to Gibran.

Soon the smell of village smoke is strong, and I see the glimmer of the moat through the trees at the forest's edge. Then I see the thatched roofs, and the bare ground about the houses, bright beneath the moon.

Gibran's eyes are glazed, and his face is wet with sweat.

I help him into his canoe, and before I step in I turn and take Ashok's face between my hands. I press my forehead to his. Something passes between us – something sweet and anguished; and he whines and licks my wrists, my hands, my face. When I get into the canoe he howls to tell his wolf-clan that I am leaving, and the sound tears at my heart. Gibran watches us, his face distraught.

I paddle us across the moat to Ahearn's place.

20

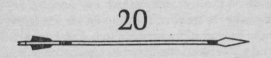

Gibran had warned me that men were wounded here, but I am not prepared for the suffering I find. The clan is in turmoil without its healer, and Tallil's prayers, though numerous and impassioned, are ineffective against raging fevers and rotting wounds. The five injured are in Ahearn's house, and his sons have meanwhile moved to another house to live. Hrothi too is here, lying near the place that was Ahearn's. The healer is dying, drowning in the fluid and blood that gathers in his lungs. His breathing is like Nolwynn's in her last days.

I make a bed for Gibran in Ahearn's house, and for seven days I look after all the injured. The clan helps, when they see that something can be done; they help me wash the sick and change their soiled furs, and gather the herbs and roots I need from the forest. They watch as I prepare the poultices and medicines, and peer over my shoulder as I anoint the wounds with ointments, and bind them up with healing leaves.

At the end of the seven days they speak courteously with me, but I know they mistrust me. They come to look on Gibran's fearful wounds, and they go away muttering about the viciousness of beasts. Some of the men talk of a hunt to annihilate the wolves. Gibran too hears the whispers. One day, while I am washing him, he says: "Fear not, Tanith. I will speak with the clan as soon as I am well. I will say that Ashok only defended you, and that afterwards on our way here he slept near me to keep me warm, and guarded us. I will tell them that the wolves have a gentle side, and are wise. There will be no hunt. I swear that, on my life."

Still I fear, and I wish with all my heart that I could howl wolf howls, and warn my kinsfolk to go to a far territory.

My fears lessen as the wounded men get well, for the time is close when I can leave. Gibran knows this, and grows restless. We have not talked much, for I have made him stay in his sleeping-furs, and we have had no privacy. I have made up my old bed near to Hrothi's, so I will know if he awakes and has need of me. And I am restless, too, and sharp with Gibran when he tries to be loving with me. I hate myself for causing him pain, yet I cannot change. I hurt him to stop him loving me, and tell him that I shall soon be gone.

"Stay a while longer," he says, this evening of the seventh day. He lies in his sleeping-furs, scooping up his broth with the bronze and jewelled spoon that Ahearn gave me. "My wounds are almost healed. Come with me to my father's clan tomorrow, stay with us there until the next new moon. Please."

"I want to go back to the wolves," I say. I am feeding Hrothi, though he takes only a few sips of warm broth, and even that bubbles in his throat and is spat out. His skin is grey, and his lips and fingertips are blue.

"Why are you so determined to cut me off?" asks Gibran, and there is an angry edge to his voice. He can speak freely now, because this afternoon the other men returned to their own families, and we are alone with Hrothi. "Give me a chance, Tanith, else you will always wonder whether or not you could have lived happily with me."

"I will never be happy with people," I say. "There is something shadowed in them, that I cannot trust. They smile at me with their mouths, but their eyes are full of hate. If they were wolves they would growl and snarl, and I would know exactly what is in their hearts. I have been too long with wolfish truth to live with people now. Besides, the wolves are my true kinsfolk, and it is them I love."

"True kinsfolk?" he cries. "Did a she-wolf give birth to you? You live in a dream, Tanith! Your mother was a dark-head. You were born in a human village, like the rest of us. You lived with wolves for a few seasons when you were a child, that is all. I understand your affection for wolves, but I am weary of your obsession with them. Sometimes I wonder if you *are* possessed, and Tallil was right to exorcise you."

My hands shake as I put down Hrothi's bowl on the

dirt floor. I rise and go outside, ignoring Gibran as he calls my name. I sit on the edge of the moat, and long for Ashok.

Gibran comes and sits by me.

"I am sorry, Tanith. With all my heart, I am sorry. I did not mean it, about your being possessed. I have never believed that, not for a moment. I said those words out of anger, out of frustration with you. I am sorry. I have been so hurt, these past few days, by your coldness towards me. I was trying to hurt you in return."

"You did. It was a clever cut, even for a warrior."

"I am sorry. If I could, I would wipe those words out as if they had never been. But I cannot, and I suppose they will forever be in the air dividing us. Always, something keeps us apart. On that awful night when they exorcised you, I tried to stop them. I would have killed, to prevent what they did to you. But they held me back, tied me to the fence on the far side of the village. I heard your cries, and could not come to you. And even when we *are* together, we are torn apart by words, or wolves. Oh, Tanith. Why is there always strife between you and me? I am trying to win you, and making a hellish mess of it."

"I am sorry, too," I say.

"Why? Because I try to win you, or because I make a mess of it?"

His question amuses me, though I leave it unanswered. When he puts his arm around me, I do not pull away.

"I think it is not our destiny to be together," I say. "Whether my kinsfolk are dark-heads or wolves, you and I are from opposite worlds."

"I saw opposite worlds meet," he replies, "when you

and Ashok said farewell. I would give my fighting arm to have that tenderness from you."

We are silent, watching night descend. From deep in the forest a wolf howls.

"Your kinsman is going hunting," Gibran says.

"Kinswoman," I say. "It is Shula. And she is not hunting; she is calling me. Listen. There are the cubs. And that last long howl is Ashok's."

"When will you go back to them, Tanith?"

"As soon as Hrothi no longer needs me."

"I need you, too."

"Your wounds are almost healed."

"Only the wounds you can see. If you listened to my heart, you would hear it throb with pain and longing, saying your name over and over: *Ta-nith, Ta-nith.*"

I laugh, and he lifts my chin and kisses me. Again the wolves howl. They sound mournful, and I am anxious for them. But Gibran's hand moves across my face and throat and strokes away my fears, and his warmth is good.

21

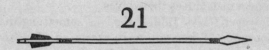

Hrothi died this night. He is burned now, his ashes blown by the wind into the dark.

Gibran sits by me at the funeral feast, and offers me roasted pork from his plate. "You have eaten nothing in this feast, Tanith," he says. I look away; I cannot bear his smile. It conquers me, and I do not wish to be conquered.

"I am not hungry," I say.

"You have eaten little these past few days," he says. "You have been too occupied looking after the sick. But see – they are all well now, thanks to you, and into the food like bees into a honey-pot. Are you not proud that your skills have made us well? The clan is grateful to you."

I say nothing. I do not believe him.

Tallil stands, and the clan is silent. The priest looks sternly at me. I bend my head. Gibran's fingers steal across my thigh, and his hand enfolds my hand. He squeezes gently, lending me his strength.

"Your remedies for our wounded were true and good, wolf-woman," says Tallil, his voice loud in the sudden quiet. The fire crackles, and a night-hawk screeches outside. I look at the faces of the people around me. Their eyes are cold.

Tallil continues, "We are thankful that you brought our pledge-son home, and stayed to help us."

There are whispers when he mentions the pledge-son, and a man curses the wolves.

"However," says Tallil, "there is something that we cannot ignore. When you were exorcised, Tanith, wolf-spirits were driven out of you. But the spirits returned, and you welcomed them. They sent you back to the wolves, and when the pledge-son went to look for you he was viciously attacked. We are afraid that if you stay any longer, you will draw the wolves to our clan, and they will kill us all."

Gibran rises, his hand strong about mine, drawing me up beside him. He still wears a strip of hide above his eye, and he cannot move freely yet, because of painful scars. But he stands tall, and I know why the clan honours him.

"When you talk about evil spirits, you are talking about your own fears," Gibran says. "Tanith was not driven to the wolves by spirits: she chose to go to them, because they are more trustworthy than we are."

There are scornful guffaws, but Gibran ignores them.

"I was not attacked by a wolf," he says. "The wolves did not even growl when I went into their territory and spoke with Tanith. Only when I was angry with her, when I shouted and shook her, the chief wolf challenged me. He could have killed me easily, for in the fight I dropped my knife; but he only warned me against hurting her, and let me go. And afterwards, when Tanith came with me through the forest, that same wolf came with us and guarded us, and he slept by me to keep me warm. It is folly to speak of the wolves as savage. In truth, they have more restraint than warriors."

There are mutterings of disbelief, and an old man calls out: "Your voice is only one, pledge-son, against tens of thousands of voices through more seasons than we can count. Always the wolf has been feared for its savagery and its killing hate. This we know, have always known since bards first told stories and sang songs. Though you are our pledge-son and we love and honour you, I think the wolf-woman has you under her spell."

"We have been through this bewitchment foolishness," says Gibran. "It was proved to be a lie, born out of jealousy. I am not bewitched. I have seen things you have not seen, that is all. As has Tanith. It is Tanith's voice and mine, for the wolves. If you banish her, you banish me."

"Those are not wise words, pledge-son," warns Tallil. "If you force us to cast you out, you force us to break a solemn pledge. Tanith has banished herself, because she committed a crime when she rejected our exorcism. She is no longer of the house of Ahearn, or of this clan. She no longer wears the red headband of Ahearn's house. If you choose to go with her, that is your concern, and you must speak with your father of it. But remember that by the laws you may be released from the pledge only in one of two ways: if you marry, in which case you return to your father's house; or if you are named chieftain of your father's clan, though that is unlikely because you are the youngest son."

"I am released of the pledge," says Gibran, putting his arm about my waist. "I will marry Tanith, and you will be relieved of us both."

"As you wish," says Tallil, and his teeth glint in the firelight. "You take the woman, and leave us to deal with her wolves."

"I would speak with you alone," I whisper to Gibran.

But he does not hear. He grips Tallil by his robe, and forces him against the wall. There is a stunned silence. No one has dared to touch the priest like this, before. Gibran is shaking with rage. But he speaks softly, slowly, as if choosing his words with great care. "Kill the wolves, and I swear that I shall renounce this clan," he says. "I will blame you for the broken pledge. And my father's men will come and set fire to your houses and your fields, in lawful retribution. This I swear on my life, and on my father's name."

No one moves or speaks. Gibran releases the priest, then takes my hand. He is breathing heavily, and his hand hurts mine, he holds me so hard. Suddenly he turns and walks out, pulling me after him.

When we are outside Gibran takes me to the house where he lives. It is smaller than Ahearn's, and there are more beds along the walls because his foster parents have seven children. Inside the house he lets go of my hand and begins taking clothes from a wooden chest and putting them on his bed. Fine tunics he throws down, and leather belts with jewelled clasps, and fur cloaks. He ties it all into a bundle with one of the belts, drawing the leather tight because he is furious, and stands looking at me.

"Are you ready to go?" he says.

"We must talk," I say.

"What about?"

"I do not want to be your wife, Gibran."

He swears softly, and drops the bundle on the floor. For a while he stands looking at the cold firepit, and his face is hard.

"You tell me one thing with your kisses, and another with your words," he says. "Make up your mind, woman, else I shall make a huge mistake, and a desperate fool of myself."

"My mind has always been made up. And if kisses are a marriage pledge, then you have several wives. I have never deceived you, Gibran. I have always told you what is in my heart, but you will not listen. Try to understand me. The only happiness I have is with the wolves. Marriage to you would alter that."

He looks at me, and his face is warm again. "It would alter your life, Tanith, but it will also give you pleasure. I swear I would honour you, would love only you, would be true and gentle with you. This is no sudden thing I ask. Always I have loved you. I cannot believe that you are not drawn to me. Tell me you find me ugly and repulsive, and that you have never wanted me."

I shake my head, and look away from his beautiful eyes and mouth. "I want you," I say, "but I want peace too, and the harmony of my other life. At the moment what I have with you does not cancel that out."

"I would never stop you visiting the wolves, Tanith. I promise you that. Just tell me that you will be my wife, and we will leave now."

"Do not push me, Gibran, else I shall only run."

"Then I will tell the clan that I am going on a visit to my father and will return in three days. Come with me, Tanith, and meet my people. When I come back here, you are free to return to the wolves, if that is what you wish. I will live here with this clan as pledge-son, and you will know where I am if you should ever change your mind. Can I offer you a fairer thing than that?"

"It is a fair agreement," I say, and he grins and picks up his bundle of clothes again. He kisses my cheek, and we go back to the funeral feast. I wait outside while Gibran speaks briefly with Tallil, and then we leave.

22

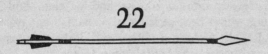

The forest is quiet between our two villages. I miss the howling of the wolves. The earth is too quiet, as if something ominous hangs over it. Gibran knows I am uneasy, and holds my hand as we walk.

The moon is full, and its silver beams drench the paths we walk, and turn the shadows blue about us. It is so bright that we can see each leaf fallen on our path, each stone and twig. The only sounds are our soft boots treading on the earth, and our breathing, for it is a long way to Gibran's place and we walk fast. Gibran carries his bundle slung across his shoulder, and will not admit that it rubs on his cuts not yet wholly healed. He is the warrior again, stalwart and tough, on his way home. But every now and again he looks down at me, and his smile is all tenderness.

"You will like my clan," he says. "My father is old now, but he has a twinkle in his eye, and he got himself a young wife last winter to warm him at night. I know you will be welcome there, Tanith. My father is a generous man, peaceable and homely. We are farmers and herdsmen, and our cows are the finest in these lands. We spend more time beating iron into ploughshares than into swords."

"Did it grieve you to leave your peaceful home and live with Ahearn's warriors?" I ask.

"I grieved at first, when I was only five summers old. But I grew to honour Ahearn and his clan. And I like fighting, when the foe is equal to us. Do not frown so, love. I shall become a farmer and do battle only with milking buckets and brutal cows, I swear."

I laugh, and we walk in silence for a while, easy in each other's company.

It is morning when we reach his village. I see grassy pastures and a wheatfield. There is no moat about the houses, only a stone wall topped by wooden spikes. There are no skulls on them. As we arrive a gate is taken down, and boys and girls drive out the cows that have been kept safe inside during the night. The herd pours out, lowing, and shying away from us. The children wave and shout greetings when they see Gibran. He waves back, then takes my hand again, and we go through the gateway into the village.

It is about the same size as Ahearn's, only there is more ground between the houses and the wall, for they have more animals to protect at night. A woman comes out of one of the houses, sees Gibran and me, and calls to someone inside. With cries of delight she runs to us, and hugs Gibran close. He kisses her on both cheeks, and they stare at one another for a time, smiling.

"What has happened to you, Gibran?" she asks, suddenly serious. "What has put these scratches on your hands and arms, and that hurt on your eye? I think they are not battle-scars."

"They are," he says, laughing a little. "I did battle with a wolf a while ago." He turns and puts out a hand to me. "Come, Tanith," he says, "meet my sister."

Me too she greets warmly, hugging me close so I smell the herbs in her garments and in her hair. She kisses my cheeks and does not care that my hair is black and that my race is enemy to hers. We hear a glad shout, and an old man comes hobbling towards us. Gibran races to meet him. They clasp one another, and Gibran picks him up, spins him around in a circle, and kisses his bald head. All the clan is out here now, to meet us.

Gibran's father, whose name is Finbar, beams as he embraces me. I am overwhelmed by the delight and welcome of this place. It is all a blur: a child brings me a bowl of warm milk to drink, and another brings a gift of whortleberries, while all about us chickens flap and hound-dogs bark. A woman presses a beautiful scarlet girdle into my arms, and someone else brings me shoes. Gibran too is lavished with gifts, and after a while, seeing that I am confused and speechless, he takes me into his father's house.

It is quiet in here, and dark after the fierce sun. His father makes us sit on low stools and brings us ale to drink in horn cups. I am thirsty, and he fills mine twice before I begin to feel satisfied. I relax, tired because I have not slept all night. It is very restful here. I smile at Gibran over the rim of my cup, and he looks on me with so much love that I am dazed by it. Light from a window streams across him, and his hair is the colour of new-cut wheat. Fine he is, so fine.

I drink my ale and listen to his voice. "And I will marry her, I hope," he is saying, "as soon as she but gives her word."

His father chuckles. "Then I had better fatten up a calf, ready for the wedding feast," he says.

A woman standing beside him looks at me, her eyes sparkling. She is not much older than I. "You will give your word," she says to me. "This place will beguile you with its charm, Tanith. It did me. And I married old Finbar here, and I have not regretted it."

There are many people in the room, and after a while Gibran tells me their names. I cannot remember them. I notice the three young women of a dark-haired clan, but I do not feel kinship with them. Their hair is glossy and long, and I am ashamed of my short tresses. I see a young man Gibran's age, and he looks so like Nolwynn that I am shocked. I realise that he is Ahearn's first-born, the pledge-son he exchanged for Gibran. I wonder if he knows his father is dead. Perhaps, since he has Nolwynn's gentle nature, he does not care about his warrior father. He never came to visit him.

Gibran has several brothers and sisters, all older than himself. His brothers still live in their father's house, with their wives and children. I count fifteen piles of furs in here, and wonder where I shall sleep. I see Gibran's eyes on me. I think he reads my thoughts, and I blush and drink more ale.

Finbar's new wife, Freya, takes me for a walk out to the fields, and I am grateful for the fresh air, though the sun dazzles me and makes my head ache. Freya chats easily, non-stop, like the magpies. As we walk through the pastures, the cows watch us with their huge, tranquil eyes. I giggle, for I cannot imagine Gibran milking them. Freya thinks I am amused at something she has said, and is spurred on to more entertaining stories about her family. Yet I enjoy her company, for no woman has talked to me like this before, apart from Nolwynn. I shelter my eyes with my hands from the blazing sun, and pay her more attention.

"And that is what my brothers were like," she says. "What is your family like, Tanith?"

"I do not know the name of my clan," I say. "I ... I wandered from home, I think, when I was little. Ahearn found me in the forest, and kept me for an adopted daughter."

Her fair eyebrows rise, and she looks impressed. "A chieftain's daughter, you are. No wonder Gibran wants you for a wife. You are of high standing in your clan."

"That is not why he wants me," I say, and she smiles suddenly, her teeth even and gleaming in the light.

"I know that," she says slyly, "by the way he looks at you."

We continue our walk, and she shows me the river that runs at the bottom of their fields. They go fishing here for trout and salmon, and here the clan gets its water. I enjoy the clean grasses and open fields, and the freedom from the treachery of the marshes. And I enjoy the openness in Freya's face, her way of looking straight at me without any hint of distrustfulness or fear.

That evening, while Freya and the other women cook the feast, I sit with Gibran on the edge of the cow pastures and tell him a new thing that I have in my heart.

"Freya thinks that I am the adopted daughter of Ahearn," I say. "Does she know that I was hated by his clan, that they think I am evil, and exorcised me?"

"No. They know nothing of you," he says, "save what you and I have said today. I have told them nothing more than that you are of the house of Ahearn and that I favour you." He puts his hand upon my cheek and turns my face towards him. His fingers are gentle on my skin. "My father thinks you are a suitable wife for me," he says. "He says there is strength in you, and that you will soon tame me."

"I would not tame a wolf, let alone a man."

"But you already have, Tanith. You have totally enslaved me." His lips are warm on mine, and taste of berries and honey. A long time he kisses me, and he lies me on the grass with him, and strokes my hair. His hand wanders down, and I hold it in my own to keep it safe against my waist.

"Do you mind," I say, "if we do not tell them of the wolves?"

"Have you forsworn them?"

"No! No, not for as long as I live. But I like your people here, and I do not want them to be suspicious of me."

"They will not be. They like you well. So there is a chance, then, for me?"

"A chance? For what?"

"Marriage, Tanith."

"Oh, I think not. My heart is still elsewhere."

"Then I shall have to change my methods of wooing you." The sunset is vivid gold on him, and he has a wicked gleam in his eye. He growls suddenly, and bares his teeth, and throws himself on me. He licks my face and neck, and I am laughing so much that I hardly have the strength to push him off. But I do, and he lies beside me and whines and howls so loudly that people come out of the houses to see· what is happening, and the cows gallop off in terror. I cover his mouth with my hand to silence him, and he bites me softly. I think of Ashok, and sorrow washes over me.

I lay my head on Gibran's chest and watch the sun set, while his fingers move slowly in my hair.

"You are strange, wolf-woman," he says, sighing.

As we go back to the house I hear a sound that I have longed to hear all day: it is the howling of a wolf.

I say to Gibran, "It is my kinsman, Ashok."

He laughs, but his eyes are curious. "Is that so?" he says. "And what is your kinsman telling you?"

"That a lone man passes through the borders of his territory," I say, "and is following the river to this place. He will be here before the moon is over the trees."

Gibran shakes his head in disbelief, and slips his arm about my neck as we walk back to his home. But our feast is hardly begun, and the round moon barely risen in the sky, when a visitor arrives.

23

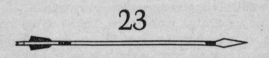

Our visitor is the bard, Camelin. It is a long time since I have seen him. If he is surprised to find me with another clan, he does not show it. Finbar's people welcome him warmly. Because he has travelled far he is given a hot bath, and dressed in fine clean garments that are their gift to him. Then he joins us for our feast. Though many of his songs are familiar to me, I have never enjoyed them so much as I do this night.

At this night's feast I am a respected guest, and I sit beside Gibran, who is at his father's right hand. Gibran and I both wear garments of linen woven fine, gifts from his clan. I have a torque of pure gold about my neck, bracelets up my arms, and a woollen cloak fixed at my right shoulder with a jewelled pin. I have bathed in Gibran's sister's house, and my skin smells of lavender oil. My cheeks are reddened with the herb called ruam, and my hair is combed until it shines. Gibran gave me a saffron-coloured headband. I feel awkward in it, for it is the colour of his father's house, and I do not think I have the right to wear it. But Gibran thinks I have, and often he looks at me, smiling, and honours me by offering me choice pieces of roast meat. He slices the meat and gives it to me on the blade of his feasting-knife, the one that hangs from his belt in a leather sheath. This knife is new, and replaces the one I forced from his hand when he fought Ashok. I take the meat from it, and look into Gibran's eyes, and my kinsfolk seem another world away.

On Finbar's other side sits the bard. Although he is elderly now, he is still spirited and fiery, and an impressive actor. His face changes with each poem that he tells; he weeps with one breath and laughs with the next, and has us all so rapt that we forget to eat.

The feast is lengthy, interrupted as it is with so much merriment and so many entranced silences while we listen to Camelin's words, but at last the food is cleared away and we all sit around the fire and tell stories. Gibran's sister tells a funny tale about her first quarrel with her husband, and how she hit him so hard that he fell in a cauldron of warm broth. When she has finished her story, she looks at Gibran and says: "Tell us your story, brother."

"I do not have one," he says.

"Of course you do!" she says. "You fought a wolf, and won. Is that not a grand tale to tell?"

Gibran flushes deeply, and glances at me. "It is not so grand a tale," he says, but all the clan is in an uproar, imploring him to tell it. So he does, slowly at first, but warming to it.

"There was a time when I fought a wolf," Gibran says, and the clan is very quiet. "He was huge, large as a pony, and strong. I trespassed in his territory and angered him. He growled, warning me that the place where I stood was his, and there I had no right to be.

"But I am a warrior, so I said to the wolf, 'This forest is all mine, and I walk where I please, for I am a man and you are only a beast.' And the wolf growled again and bared his fangs at me. So I showed him that I am a man and a warrior: I fought him, bare-handed, without my knife or sword. It was a good fight, full of courage; and the victor was excellent and noble. So noble was he that, at the end, when he had my throat between his teeth and could have killed me, he walked away. 'I give you back your life,' he said to me, 'because you are only a man, and I am a beast.'"

I look at Camelin. His eyes are fixed on Gibran's face, and he is smiling a little. Then his gaze shifts to me. I wonder if he realises that I have lived with wolves again, and that it was because of me that Gibran fought. I suspect he does know: he reads people's hearts, this bard.

Finbar is delighted with the story, and slaps Gibran's shoulder. "Not a bad tale, my son," he says. "A mix of truth and parable, I think. Now tell us another story, Camelin. Is there any news of other clans? What happened to that fierce wife of the chieftain who lives in the Mountains of Mornn?"

"Ah – that woman!" says the bard, and he chuckles

in his deep voice, then frowns and shakes his head. "She made his life a misery, until ..."

Many stories the bard tells: stories of battles fought, of marriages and births, victories and shames, heroes and fools. We laugh at some of the tales, recognising our own foibles. The bard's honesty is relentless. Many a man has had his reputation ruined because Camelin heard of some misguided thing he did. It is for this reason that he is so respected and well treated: if a chieftain is rude to him, or stingy with his hospitality, the whole world hears of it. We all are topics for his stories.

When the story-telling is finished pitchers of ale are passed around, and cold meat from the feast is brought back on large platters. I am not used to so much food, for I ate frugally with the wolves, and the feast and the ale and a sleepless night last night all combine in a great weariness. I lean against Gibran, and listen to the fire crackling and the voices of the clan. It is warm near the flames, and I doze for a while with Gibran's arm close about me, my head on his shoulder. I am woken by music, the tranquil, lovely sounds of the bard's lyre, and his voice singing. I sit up straight, with my arms about my knees, and listen, enraptured.

Oh, how splendid are the songs! They fly me to another world, enflame me, transfigure me. And I think that one day I too shall be a bard, a singer-poet, and give to others this marvellous gift that he gives me. I am filled with longing to sing as he sings, with that passion, that power, that grief, that ecstasy.

Gibran slips his arm about me again and draws me close to him. He caresses me and whispers love words in my ears, not caring that his clan sees, that the old ones smile at us. New longings sweep through me. I close my eyes, lost in the beauty of the songs and in Gibran's warmth and tenderness.

When I open my eyes again, I see Ashok, standing between me and the fire. He is silver-drenched in moonlight, blue and cool against the flames, and his eyes shine and are filled with kinship and love. I cry out, and lean forward to caress his milk-white chin; but he is gone, vanished. I look at the dirt floor. There is nothing there but boot prints, and the edge of Gibran's cloak.

Gibran watches me, his eyes questioning.

"What is it, love?" he says. "You called out."

"Ashok was here," I say.

At that moment there is a howl from far in the forest. It is a warning-howl, telling of hunters and peril.

"I must go!" I cry. I interrupt Camelin's song. The people all look at me, their faces bewildered and alarmed.

I try to stand, but Gibran restrains me, gently, forcefully. "You were dreaming," he says. "Sit down."

I do, but I am uneasy, for I have glimpsed, through the window-hole, the round and dazzling moon. "It is Ashok's moon," I say, "and I must be with him."

"No, all is well," says Gibran, stroking my cheek. But my nerves are jangled, and I have no peace. The songs no longer enchant me. Gibran's hand steals under my cloak, and I pull away from him.

"Something is wrong," I say. "Ashok is telling me."

"Hush," he says, irritated. "You disturb the songs, Tanith."

In that moment of quiet, I hear another howl. A long high howl it is, a cry of fear and agony. It hangs in the night, lingering, and is suddenly cut short. Pain tears through me. I scream, and look down at my hands. They are covered in blood. There is blood and darkness everywhere, and pain, and howls so terrible –

"Tanith!" It is Gibran, standing up with me, shouting. All the clan is watching us, and the children have backed away, afraid. "Tanith! What is wrong with you? *Tanith!*"

Pain again, an awful pain that tears right through me, from my left side to my right, like a knife in my bowels. I scream and stagger, and Gibran holds my arms and forces me to look at him.

"What is wrong, my love?" he cries, afraid. "Are you poisoned?"

But it is not Gibran I see, it is a man from Ahearn's clan, and he is slashing at me with a sword, again and again, until I am bowed down with agony and cannot breathe. My throat is cut; blood pours over my tongue.

Someone holds me, binds me, and I howl and lash out at him. I smell fur and flesh burning. There is a shout, and something hits me across the face, hard. I am stunned. I fall back, and human arms hold me up. Gibran is staring at me, his face bleeding where his cheeks are scratched. I am horrified: who has done this thing to him?

I hear the wolves in the forest whining and baying, howling out their grief and agony. The noise fills the room, and I think Ashok has come back in a fury, and I cannot understand why the clan does not flee in terror, or why they stand and stare at me as if I am demented. I see Gibran's face again, distorted by pain, tears mingling with the blood. He is shaking his head and backing away from me.

151

Anguish tears me apart. "Ashok!" I cry. I scratch and bite and fight until I am let go, then I flee from the fire-warmed house, the human company. I run so fast that it is as if Ashok himself runs with me, urging me on. The cold night rushes past, grasses and low branches slashing at me, the forest flashing by like a dark, wild dream. All like a dream this is, a terrible dream from which I must awaken, or my world is destroyed.

On and on I run, until breathing is torture. Still I run, barely aware of the grey dawn breaking. Sweat drips into my eyes, and my dress hinders me. Exhausted, I stumble, fall, then force myself on again. Pain engulfs me; I go through it, past it, driving my body on and on. My heart and my spirit pour out across the dawn, pour out with Ashok's blood across the earth, leap with his spirit into the wind and the growing light and –

At last I am at the place of Ahearn's village, on the forest side of the moat. Torches still blaze on the shore, and the morning is torn with men's shouting and laughter. On the ground, covered in blood and dust, and charred with fire, are the bodies of the wolves. Many wolves there are. They are stretched out in a row along the curved shore of the moat. I walk past them, looking at them, and silence falls. Only the flaming torches move in the wind, and I.

I see two wolves that I have met as they crossed Ashok's territory. There are three I do not know. Then there is Zeki, her lovely fur matted with blood. She has been run through with an arrow, and slit from her throat to her tail. Zaal is next to her, his head half severed. Then a wolf who is a stranger to me, burned alive and still panting. And Shula, my beautiful Shula, her eyes sliced across with a knife and her head crushed, and her white throat black with blood. She is dead, dead. And then Ashok –

Oh, Ashok! Ashok, wolf my father! I kneel beside him and put my arms about his neck and lift his huge head and hold it against my heart, and I gaze into his eyes, still wide but dull like overshadowed moons; and I howl and cry. I feel his blood seep through my clothes, and I touch my fingertips to it and lick them so that a part of him may become a part of what I am. I kiss his nose and his ears and his beautiful eyes, and lie him down again. I stand up and examine the other wolves. Ten more there are, but none I know.

Glancing up, I see the men of Ahearn's clan on the other side of the moat, on the ground outside Ahearn's house. Their faces are proud, gloating; they look on me as if I am mad and they have punished me for it, and now they will be rid of me. Tallil stands there, swinging his incense and useless charms, chanting a prayer of protection against me and my evil wolf spirits. Something breaks in me: the last cord that ties me with humankind.

"Pray well, priest!" I cry. "Pray with all your might, for you grieve the gods and the earth, and you destroy the great and perfect dream they had for it. You are mad! All of you! You warriors who stand there with bloodied hands, smiling and satisfied, as if you had done some great and mighty deed! And what is it you have done? Slain beasts that never gave you harm! Gone out with arrows and spears and hate against beings who sought only to dwell in peace. Oh, great warriors you are! You slice a child in two with a sword, and call yourselves brave! You fall upon a sleeping village in the sun, slaughter everyone, and think it proves what fine and noble men you are! Oh, how your gods must weep and lament over you! I swear, there is more virtue and wisdom in the wolves, than there is in you! Yet they have died, because of your stupidity – your terrible, futile, arrogant stupidity!

"And you, priest – you, who claim to know the minds and the hearts of the gods! You are the most ignorant of all! Do you not ever listen to your own teachings? You say the earth was made for us, that the animals and trees and everything alive was given into our hands, for us to guard and protect. Yet you stand by and approve this destruction! You let them brutalise the beings we were meant to nurture, and violate the very lives we were meant to sustain! Are your brains dead, and your hearts with them? Ashok understood the plan, the great giving and taking, the harmony! But not you! Not you!"

"You are possessed!" shouts Tallil, furious, shaking his finger at me. "I warn you, wolf-woman! Go now, or you will suffer the same fate as your wolves!"

"Oh, I will leave!" I cry. "Never again shall I walk with humans, or enter your dwellings. I renounce everything I ever had that binds me to you!"

I turn and walk away from them.

The forest is ringing with the first songs of the birds. I go back to Ashok's den, for it is the only home I know. Men's footprints are outside, and deep furrows in the dirt where something has been dragged, and claw marks, and blood. Blood everywhere. Burning torches have been flung inside the den, and the smell of smoke still hangs in the air. But new upon the dust, clear upon the signs of strife, are fresh wolf prints, not dragged across, but made by steady, quiet paws. I stare at them, not understanding, and for a glorious moment I think that I have made a mistake, that Ashok still lives. I sense a presence in the trees, beyond the den, but see only shadows shifting in the morning wind.

I gaze at my bloodstained arms, at the ravaged earth in front of the den, and despair floods over me.

There is a movement in the dimness. I look up and see a wolf. My eyes are blurred, and at first I do not recognise him. Then he wags his tail and whines, and I know.

"Kalasin!" I say. "I had forgotten you, in all the madness."

He comes over, hesitant because there is blood in this place and on me. I kneel and put my arms about his neck. His fur is warm, soft and alive, and smells of the vital earth.

"Tell me, wolf my brother," I say, "when we are at the end of all our hope, what is there then?"

I draw back from him a little, and see his eyes. Luminous and deep they are, steady as the moon in a stormy sky, lamps shining in all my darkness, like other eyes I loved.

A long time I sit with him in the dirt. He licks my face, and nuzzles me, whining. I hear him pant, feel his warmth, his strength; and slowly peace comes. It is wolf-peace: a belief in renewal, in the morning after the night. It is the silent certainty that nothing is ever finished, nothing lost, nothing gone – not for as long as life ebbs and flows, and the seasons spin their beginnings and endings across the enduring earth.

I take off the saffron-coloured headband that a stranger

gave to me, and place it on the bloodied dust in front of Ashok's den.

And I go away with the wolf, my kinsman.

24

I lie in the field outside Kalasin's den, and watch the
distant river shimmering through the grass. Beside me
stretches Raida, her belly round with unborn cubs, her
eyes half closed as she dozes. Kalasin sits licking his
paws, and I roll over and gently tug his tail. He springs
away, crouches low, and grins, daring me to wrestle him.
Suddenly he sits bolt upright, his ears pricked towards
the river.

A man comes, walking with a staff, a lyre across his
back. It is Camelin. I jump up and start running through
the grass to meet him, Kalasin bounding with me. He
snaps at my hands as we run, playfully, and once he
dashes in front of me and we tangle together, falling in

the grass, yelling and yelping. I stand up and tell him to wait. Then I brush the grasses from my frayed dress and walk on to meet the bard.

Camelin is resting on a stone beside the water. He has taken off the lyre, and the heavy bag he had across his shoulder. He holds out something to me.

"Greetings, wolf-woman," he says, as I take the gift. It is a dress, grey and soft as the fur of wolves.

"Greetings, Camelin," I say. "Thank you. I need another one."

"So I see." His eyes sparkle, and his smile is good to look upon, for we are friends by now. "And I see you survived the winter storms," he adds.

"Not easily, though," I reply. "Many bitter days and nights I was grateful for the boots and furs you brought to me. And I was thankful for the flints. It was good to have a fire at times, and to eat roasted meat."

"I looked for you, when the snows were deep. The den over there was abandoned."

"We wandered around the winter hunting-grounds, following the deer. There were not many hares and smaller prey."

I sit on the sun-warmed stone beside the bard, and am keenly aware of his shrewd eyes watching me.

"Are you not eager to hear news?" he asks.

"I am," I say, "if it is the news I want to hear."

"I cannot sift the good news from the bad, Tanith. I tell what I have seen and heard. And I have heard vital things about Ahearn's clan, and the pledge-son."

"Tell me your news, then," I say.

"I heard that there was major strife within that clan, between the pledge-son and the rest of them. It is said that Gibran swore revenge if Ahearn's clan killed the wolves. When he found that many of the wolves were dead, Gibran disowned Ahearn's people, and blamed them for breaking the pledge. But when he went home to his father and tried to persuade Finbar to burn Ahearn's village in retribution, the old man refused. He said that the pledge-son laws are more binding than personal vows, and he sent Gibran back to Ahearn's clan. And Finbar was right: Gibran was bound to remain with Ahearn's people, or he would have broken the pledge-son laws himself and caused war between the two clans. Finbar's people would have been wiped out. So Gibran stayed as pledge-son, though his life was hellish difficult, all winter. He lived in a hut on the other side of the moat, but near enough so that they could not say he had deserted them.

"Then old Finbar, on his death-bed two full moons ago, named Gibran as the new chieftain of his clan. It released the son from the pledge, and brought him with honour back to his own people. There was discord with the oldest brother, who expected to be chieftain, but Finbar's word was binding. Gibran is a worthy leader of the clan, I hear, and a man of peace. I was his guest, a few nights ago. He did not speak of the winter's happenings, but he talked of you."

I study a pattern worked into the hem of the dress, and realise it is the new chieftain's sign: arrows, not straight and hard, but softly wound about each other like vines around trees.

"He gave me the dress to give to you," says Camelin. "And he gave me a message for you. The new chieftain asks if you will stand with him in a wedding-feast, and live with him in his father's house."

"I cannot," I say.

"He will be grieved, Tanith," says the bard, his voice gentle. "Do not blame him for failing to avenge your wolves. He was tangled in promises far older and stronger than any vows he made to you. And now he bears the responsibilities of chieftainship. But he says he will wait for you, and will take no other woman."

"I cannot go to him. I, too, have made vows, Camelin. I will not enter the houses of men again. Tell him to come to me, and we will live together with the wolves."

"Is that a fair thing to ask of a chieftain?" says the bard, and sighs.

I look out across the sun-kissed fields, and slowly the pain in me subsides.

"Raida will have her cubs soon," I say. "Perhaps this very morning. I am looking forward to it, Camelin. It is a lovely time, the spring: all things are born anew."

The bard reaches into his bag and takes out a parcel wrapped in white linen. He opens it, spreading the cloth across his knees. Berry pies are there, smelling sweeter than the spring grasses. He offers one to me, and we eat together.

"Do you still make up songs, Tanith?" he asks.

"All the time," I reply. I hesitate a moment, gathering my courage. I have an idea precious to me, that I want to put to him. "I have been thinking," I say "if I were to teach you some of the songs I have made would you sing them to men and women in the clans?"

"What are they about?"

"About the wisdom and the gentleness of wolves."

"And do you think people would listen, Tanith?"

"They will, if you sing them. I had a dream, once, that made me afraid. It was a vision of the far future. I saw that the wolves will always be hunted, over and over, until they are no more. I want my songs sung, Camelin. People will listen, if you sing them, for your voice carries power."

"I tell you in truth, they will not listen. They fear the wolves, and they despise themselves for being afraid, so they are angry and go and kill the wolves. Men always destroy what they fear. They do not want to know that the thing they fear wishes them no harm – for then they will be shown to be fools, as well."

"You will not learn my songs, then?"

"Why do you not become a bard yourself, and sing them? You have a pleasing voice, I remember. On your travels the wolves could accompany you, and keep you safe. I vow, with your strange story and your songs, you would be renowned!"

"There was a time when I might have been a singer," I say, "but that time is gone."

We have finished the pies, and the bard folds the white cloth and puts it in his bag. He picks up his things again, stands, and swings the lyre across his back. He touches my hand, briefly, in farewell.

"I cannot learn your songs," he says, his eyes on Kalasin, who has smelled the pies and can no longer curb his curiosity. "We bards sing well only what we believe, what we feel in our hearts. I do not like the wolves, and I fear them; I could not sing of them. Maybe there is another, somewhere: a singer, or a teller of stories, who will share your love of wolves, and hear your words and pass them on. But I shall see you in the summer time, and bring you berry pies and news again." He hesitates, looking straight at me again, his eyes amused and wondering. "Do you know that you are a legend in these lands, Tanith? Do you know what people say of you?"

I shake my head.

"They say that you run with the wolves, and hunt, and fight with them in play. They say that you know all their secret ways, their memories and their ancient wisdom; that you hear their language and understand it, and that you can commune with them. You are Tanith of the wolves, and on winter nights when the moon is full you sit on a hill with a great wolf, and sing with him his wolf-songs. So they say."

There is a sharp yelping sound across the field, and Kalasin streaks back to Raida, barking and whining. I see his tail waving high above the long grasses, and he prances in circles in front of his den, howling in excitement and worry and ecstasy.

"The cubs!" I cry, elated, leaping off the rock, and beginning to run. "Our cubs are being born! Oh, Camelin, come and see! A whole new generation of my kinsfolk!"

The bard laughs and shakes his head, and continues on his journey along the river bank to human dwelling places. I run back through the shining field to my home in the spring-warm earth, to the birthing-place of my new kin, to the sounds of wolfish jubilation and joy.

It is a fine, fine morning.